THE INCOMER

By Graham Gaunt

THE INCOMER

THE INCOMER

GRAHAM GAUNT

PUBLISHED FOR THE CRIME CLUB BY
DOUBLEDAY & COMPANY, INC.
GARDEN CITY, NEW YORK
1982

All of the characters in this book
are fictitious, and any resemblance
to actual persons, living or dead,
is purely coincidental.

First Edition in the United States of America

ISBN: 0-385-18096-9
Library of Congress Catalog Card Number 81–43765

49291

A story for Susan, Joan, George

Where can we live but days?
Ah, solving that question
Brings the priest and the doctor
In their long coats
Running over the fields.
—Philip Larkin, "Days"

CHAPTER 1

The priest was aware that the furrow he was digging was anything but a straight line. It was a mercy therefore that the village was so quiet this dank grey morning, or people would already be criticizing him from the lane. Almost too quiet.

Above, the sky seemed draped with wet soiled altar-cloths. He paused to inspect it, finally shrugged with disappointment at there being no convincing sign of rain, and resumed his spadework. Rain on this fresh cold air would have been a welcome addition to the morning, even a kind of protection. For one thing, he thought, it would help to keep us amateur gardeners indoors and out of the way.

Today, they were releasing Taunton. And sure as death he would come straight home.

The cool air blew on Taunton's face in a way that felt new as he waited for the gates to be unlocked. The many sounds from the town sounded like a fairground concealed among those dark-hedged lanes he had known as a lad in his native village. Promising. That was the word. Full of promise, as the teachers used to say when a child did good in class. Never him, though.

"This way, *Mister* Taunton." The warder's voice held inflexibly to the word like he was in training and doing well. Showing promise.

"That's right," the gate screw said. "Mister now, eh?"

"Yes, sir," Taunton said.

"Get everything?"

"Yes, thanks, sir." Taunton half-raised his case. Everything they'd confiscated on arrival was now handed back, signed for, using a hand unbelievably cumbersome. He'd even made heavy weather of keeping the paper steady.

"Thank Gawd," the warder intoned.

"Yes. Fewer bloody forms."

And the gate opened, simple as that, into all this air. Into the street after a few yards of cobbled slope laid between parked cars with their protruding bums making walking difficult. Into the street where one or two pedestrians gave him curious guessing glances before looking at the prison, presumably checking for hullabaloo. And on to the pavement where he became like everybody else, merely one in the stream.

"He be back?" the gate screw asked, grinning.

His mate pondered a second, nodded. "Him? For sure. I'll give him . . . ten months."

"Lucky bastard. Successful appeal, weren't it?"

"Only technical. He won't stay lucky forever."

I'm out, Les Taunton thought, trying to be more pleased than amazed. Free. As a child let out of school he'd even danced, roared, cheered and run. Above all, *run*. None of this now. He could feel the eyes of the screws following him. There'd be none of that, Taunton, as they had told him time after time. And they'd simply meant none of anything. Simply do nothing, except what you're told.

He walked down the cobbled slope towards the street pavement, wondering why his lightweight case felt so heavy. He was the same person as had been arrested for that thing, now some months back, and he knew he hadn't changed. So it must be the case itself, somehow grown heavier and become different while it waited downstairs in that storeroom the screws had for prisoners' effects.

A pause to cross at the traffic lights. He was thinking, now I want to use a phone box, but there's nobody I could ring except that reporter from the *County Banner* and I'd come to dread his arrival. Pestered the life out of me. It shouldn't be allowed, all those interviews one after another and asking the same questions over and over again. Not that it got him mad, just a bit ashamed. Maybe the reporter had no idea how shameful it all had been. Or maybe he did and couldn't give a toss.

He went forward as the lights changed, a mother with a pram and a plumber humping a sackful of tools accompanying him over the pedestrian crossing. Neither even glanced his way. Having to talk when you don't want is hell. He marvelled at the sudden awareness and thought, all my life I will remember that. Only a simple idea, and yet it was more frightening than being hit or having the screws get on at you like they had. And it was still frightening, even now when he was *free* and therefore freed of the obligation of having to be talked at, clumsily forced to make up some reply that would make them go away and leave him in peace.

He paused occasionally in his progress along the pavement among the shoppers and looked in shop-windows—something he never normally did. He was a young and rather shabby man merely going home to re-enter his normal life. The joy he felt at knowing the purpose of the journey was his own private business. He was going back where he belonged, among his own. Nobody paid him attention.

CHAPTER 2

The scent of trouble had hung around the village all morning. Nothing apparent in the behaviour of people, nothing said. Dr. Clare Salford got the same smiles, the same waves on her round as always. She was offered a cup of tea by old Deller, the eldest of her three diabetics. She was invited over to his neighbour's garden to admire this autumn's best roses, grown again by Mrs. Winner, for the village show. And when driving past the school's high hedges she received her regular long look from Mr. Edgeworth, teacher who had come to educate the children in drama and physical education. Like herself, he was a recent incomer to Beckholt life.

Ever since taking over Dr. Chesterton's one-man village practise she had been aware how deeply the entire place had brooded under the publicity which attended the trial of Les Taunton. The villagers still smarted at Beckholt's notoriety, though it was probably fading now the announcement of Taunton's appeal had come through.

She drove past the wooden scout hut, swung her battered Austin down Beckholt's main road towards her surgery. At the corner, she caught a glimpse of a cassock moving fast as a blackbird along the hedges which rimmed the playing fields, but deliberately maintained her speed. The priest's arm jerked in the start of a wave, then checked as he too, recognized her deception and quickly fell in with it, walking with his usual briskness towards the village's one small housing estate. Clare snorted, her lips set thinly. He would be off to solace Jane Lang for losing her second pregnancy, in the fourth month like last time. Useless man. He'd do a lot better to talk sense into her, get her to drink less and behave—at least until the risk of miscarriage had passed. Spiritual guidance indeed!

The village's coming trouble would involve him too. Of course, Reverend Shaw Watson would plunge in without a single thought, stupid man. A youngish man like him should get the hell out of village life. And out of that ridiculous extinct so-called profession of the church. Since she had arrived months before she had encountered him face to face only a half-dozen times, and remained unimpressed. Too immersed in his theology, too wobbly in his pointless doctrines to influence people. Now, Edward Edgeworth—that was another matter. Already he was listened to, respected for his cheerfulness and dynamism. Folk were saying the headmistress, Monica James, was somewhat under his influence, and in such a short time. And she was attractive enough in her way, quite slender and blonde. Married, of course. An interesting development, but with these problems looming *that* diversion would have to be put aside.

She drove along the Lexton Road, mechanically monitoring the bungalows and houses for activity. A passing car hooted, Fogg Powell's low grey Jaguar rushing back to his farm from today's market auction. Having an aversion to sounding her motorhorn, she reached an arm out of the window and waved. He would see, in his mirror. To her surprise there were two cars and a horse-drawn cart on the road outside her surgery. An accident? She slowed, but came in sight of the three people standing talking on her gravel path. She groaned, trying hard to work up a smile of greeting, and pulled in between the low azaleas old Dr. Chesterton had planted. George Falconer, elderly and affable, smiled towards Clare's car. Eric Carnforth, not as old but more tense, nodded tightly. And of course nothing from Mrs. Horn except a slow turn of the head, signifying she was not here for time-wasting pleasantries but for serious talking.

The trouble had come, days sooner than she feared.

" 'Morning, Doctor."

" 'Morning."

The two men spoke simultaneously, but the woman waited carefully until Clare had stepped down.

" 'Morning, Dr. Salford."

" 'Morning, Mrs. Horn." Clare smiled as if appraising them. "I must say you all look singularly fit."

"We aren't here for our health, Doctor," Mrs. Horn answered, out for war.

"At least not directly," the older of the two men added. Gratefully Clare noted Mr. Falconer's attempted jocularity, a good try to neutralize Mrs. Horn's rather ominous remark. More than anybody, George Falconer could be relied on for a little moderation. But Mrs. Horn . . .

"Difficult for us all," the other man put in grimly.

"Sounds like an epidemic, Mr. Carnforth," Clare said pleasantly. "You'd better all come in."

She led the way. Jackie Hughes at the reception desk was trying not to appear too worried by the deputation.

"No messages, Doctor."

"Thank heavens, Jackie. Could you brew up, please? Then you can go. We'll leave Nurse Batsford's drug check till evening surgery."

"Yes, Doctor."

The surgery was a small affair, a mere converted ground floor. The waiting-room had been extended on Clare's insistence by a prefabricated glass-walled conservatory and decorated with garden plants. Two conjoined examination rooms led off this and a minute sluice closed that section. The doctor's consulting-room opened into the corridor where Jackie's tiny countered recess had to serve as telephone booth, filing area and patient reception. Clare had firm hopes of conning a Health Committee loan for another extension. She placed chairs for Mrs. Horn and Mr. Falconer while Jackie hurried to bring in a third.

"Don't suppose I'm allowed a pipe, Doctor?"

"Certainly not! And it's time you gave up that filthy habit." Clare pulled off her gloves and placed her handbag, sitting as if ready for a consultation. Unreasonably apprehensive, she realized with some annoyance that she was using all the practised mannerisms she adopted when deeply disturbed or uncertain. She riffled quickly through the notes on the desk while her visitors settled.

George Falconer grimaced in pretended misery at Mrs. Horn. "Doctor'll be madder at your Harry, Sarah," he jibed. "He smokes worse'n me."

Clare nodded thanks to Jackie and waited until her plump figure left the study before giving the three visitors her undivided attention. "Can I help?" She smiled with determined affability into Mrs. Horn's frosty countenance.

"You can, Dr. Salford," Mrs. Horn said. "This killer. The village doesn't want him here."

"You mean Taunton?"

"Of course I mean Taunton." Clare saw Mrs. Horn's mouth draw down at her innocent question. "Not like you to be so slow, Doctor. We don't have *that* many murderers around here."

"He's not a killer."

"*Not* a killer?" Mrs. Horn's eyes widened in utter astonishment. "Then what's he doing in prison? Or up before the judge, if it isn't for murdering Olive? Of all the things to say!"

"He's not in prison any more, Mrs. Horn. Nor in dock."

"More's the pity! We all know what he did—"

Clare interrupted as firmly as she knew how. "The law says he is innocent. He's been set free."

"How can he be innocent?" the older woman exclaimed angrily while the men exchanged glances. "The horrible man got off with a lawyer's trick, like they all seem to do these days—"

Carnforth broke in with the ease of the trained administrator. "We've been asked to call on you for your support, Doctor."

"By the village council?" Clare's counterfeit surprise took none of them in but she felt obliged to bring out the real source of this move, even if resistance displeased Mrs. Horn further.

"Well, no." Carnforth hesitated. "Just a group of us. But the feeling's very strong."

"Because we don't want murderers!"

Eric Carnforth ignored Mrs. Horn's interruption and pressed on. "George will tell you."

"Your support's been requested, Doctor," Falconer said. His tone indicated he was worried about the whole thing. "Let's put it no firmer than that."

Clare thought, I won't let them get away with *that*, and asked mildly: "Have you actually considered the matter on the council?" George Falconer was this year's chairman. Eric was the durable council clerk, who received a token stipend for this labour in addition to his regular job at a building society in Colnebridge.

"No. But we will." Carnforth's bluntness earned a pleased nod from Mrs. Horn.

"The Guild of Village Wives has already passed a resolution on Taunton," she told Clare, admonishing the two men by the comment. "We don't want him. He's a danger to everybody."

"He's innocent, Mrs. Horn." Clare's words were out before she could think.

"He's a murderer! To kill poor Olive—"

Clare said curtly, fighting for control of her temper: "What exactly are you proposing?"

"Will you support us, Doctor, or won't you?" Mrs. Horn was standing now, belligerently darting her gaze between the men and Clare. "I don't hold with shilly-shallying."

"Support *how*?"

"There's a petition," George Falconer explained.

"From whom?"

"From my Guild," Mrs. Horn snapped. "*And* the Village Confraternity."

Clare looked quizzically at Eric Carnforth. He nodded that this was so. "Last night. And there's a social club meeting about it this evening." He cleared his throat from embarrassment. "They said to ask you along."

"I'm afraid I'll be busy. What's the petition for?"

"To keep that maniac away, that's what," Mrs. Horn rasped.

"How?"

"What does it matter, *how?*"

"You really must try to think," Clare remonstrated, still trying to hold back. "*Any* way is illegal."

"Rubbish!" Mrs. Horn was practically shouting. "We don't want killers in Beckholt."

"Maybe I missed something," Clare shot back angrily. "Of what is he convicted, Mrs. Horn?"

"We all know the truth in this village!"

"Then you should have given evidence!"

"I'll tell you one thing!" Mrs. Horn's cheeks showed two red discs of heat. Her lips were thin and cyanotic from fury. "Old Dr. Chesterton would know his duty. It's a pity you don't."

"Doctor's only making constructive criticism, Sarah," George Falconer said placatingly. He had started to light his pipe, a measure of his distress at the argument.

"She's sticking up for that criminal!"

"I'm saying what the law says!" Clare answered.

"Inadmissible evidence?" Mrs. Horn jeered. "What kind of a crooked verdict's that?"

"A legal one."

"Well, then." George Falconer rose, and the other man with him. He looked mortified. "That seems all we can do here. Hope we've not interrupted your work too much, Doctor."

"Hardly at all."

"We can see that." Mrs. Horn gave Clare the full benefit of her famous stare. "Just take notice, Doctor. If you don't want to keep that killer out of this village, there are others that do."

She marched out, almost knocking Jackie's tray from her hands in the doorway. George smiled at the receptionist and pinched a biscuit by way of appeasement as he passed. Eric Carnforth left with a muttered courtesy, keeping his eyes on the carpet. Clare slumped back in her swing chair and blew a mock sigh at the appalled Jackie.

"It's all right, Jackie. Just a normal village war."

"About the surgery, Doctor?"

Clare tried a smile. Jackie lived in fear of being criticized by the village and of word getting back to Nurse Batsford, the district nurse, of whom she was especially wary.

"No. That court case."

"Les Taunton?" Jackie advanced and deposited the tray. "They say he'll come home. Everybody's up in arms."

"Silly fools," Clare said, not caring if Jackie was surprised at the remark. "Let's have some tea in peace."

CHAPTER 3

Reverend Shaw Watson was safely in the church when George Falconer's cart rattled outside. He occasionally thought of his church as haven, though unfortunately not sanctuary. After a session with Jane Lang he'd entered the vestry feeling definite relief. Her too-languid touch on his arm had been at once deliberate and provocative. Unchristian, perhaps, to accuse her mentally. After all, the distress and sorrows of yet another aborted pregnancy were unknowable to a man and, to a priest, more so than to any man alive. Yet the woman had smiled, pressed his arm, suggested he called again the following day, even adding: "Make it tennish, if it must be in the morning." Her behaviour had been deeply disturbing.

He sighed, setting to with dustpan and brush. The vestry floor was hideously uncared-for. Mrs. Oldridge, that notorious

skimper, drew her money for only token attendances. How hard
not to blame her, accuse her of idleness and dishonest acceptance of wages. The place looked untouched. Maybe the Jesuits
had the right idea—such labours were the proper and rightful responsibility of the laity. Consequently, a dirty church, a tatty
priest, were open accusations of a duty shunned. Such tellingly
silent blame never went unheeded for long.

He straightened at the sound of the cart. Night Owl blew
down her nose and something creaked, clinked. Hastily his cassock had to be found, donned, his hair combed and the dustpan
put away in the curtained alcove behind the intruding rear of
the old manual organ. Hoping he avoided seeming too flushed
he was stowing the brush away when he realized he hadn't
made it. George Falconer, embarrassed, was trying to cough a
warning. The priest reddened, though feeling an uncharitable
twinge of pleasure at having been caught out—and despite all
that alacrity.

"How do, Reverend."

"Er, just tidying a little, George. Just tidying."

"Norah Oldridge'll be mortified."

"If she finds out," Shaw put in quickly by way of erasing that
gratifying twinge of a moment ago.

Falconer grinned. "I'll say nothing, Reverend. But Norah
wants my Mary behind her. Wouldn't know what hit her." He
stepped into the narrow vestry, glancing over his shoulder into
the church, concerned like all Beckholt people at giving offence
by talking in the holy place.

"You saw Dr. Salford, then?"

"Aye." George pulled a face. "Not good."

"Really?" Shaw was suddenly more interested. He had seen
the group on his way past the surgery and guessed its intentions.
"She refused to support the petition?"

"All but threw us out. Old Sarah had a real go."

"Oh dear. What happens now?"

"Dunno. They're meeting tonight at the social club. Coming?"

He's avoiding looking straight at me, the priest realized suddenly. He's been deputed to call here. It's a—what was the

phrase—a put-up job. Probably Eric Carnforth was anxious the voluble Mrs. Horn might put her foot in it again, lead to disaffection of both priest and doctor all in one day.

"What is the meeting's precise purpose?" he asked.

"Support for the petition. They say Sergeant Sheldon will be there."

Shaw asked quickly: "In what capacity?" It was vital to know. Sheldon was the village's only policeman.

George Falconer, not to be caught easy as that, shrugged, smiling. "Haven't heard. Word is he's sympathetic to the idea, though."

"Of . . . ?"

"Of keeping Taunton out of the village."

It was as bad as he'd feared. They couldn't know what they were asking. "Then I'm afraid I can't come, George."

"Is that official?" The man's face cleared. Maybe matters would be simpler now, Shaw guessed.

"If you mean final, yes."

"I'll carry the word, then, Reverend." George grinned, at least partly with relief. "Let you get on with your tidying."

"How's the smallholding?" Shaw accompanied Falconer down the aisle and out on to the churchyard gravel. The Falconers ran a roadside stall on the village outskirts.

"Not so good."

"It might improve." Shaw had heard the local saying about the Falconer land, overpriced and underworked, but found to his unease he was writing off more and more of the village's remarks as undue cynicisms. When he first came he'd been inclined to see them as wise sayings full of country learning.

Shaw Watson watched him climb on the cart. "You do realize, George. The church must not join political acts. It's as simple as that."

"People say it's common sense, not politics, Reverend."

"Give my apologies."

"I'll do that."

Night Owl clopped away at a walk, the elderly smallholder lighting his pipe and settling down for the half mile trek out to where Mary Falconer would be preparing for the afternoon customers on their way into town. The roadside vegetable and fruit stall had become quite a landmark in the village, and a profitable venture despite George's moans. And with the notorious Taunton returning home today there would be no lack of folk eager to seize on the roadside stall as a legitimate excuse to stop and ogle Taunton's thatched cottage. Somebody's remark about all publicity being good . . .

By the church gate, Shaw felt suddenly alone. His refusal to attend was right, yet sending apologies was a definite weakness, an appeasement. A misjudgement which could only isolate the church still more. He scanned the skies, feeling a heavy drop of rain, and went back in to finish his—well, Mrs. Oldridge's—chores.

CHAPTER 4

Joe Sheldon wished he hadn't decided to phone. The conversation was becoming a nightmare. And of course it was practically the only time he'd got through to Inspector Patrick first go. Bloody typical.

"Say again," Patrick commanded irascibly, the bastard.

"Taunton, sir. Les Taunton."

"Got it. Yes?"

"He's back home today or tomorrow, sir."

"Time," Patrick intoned wearily. "Place. And, Sergeant . . . ?"

"Date, sir." Sweat itched between Sheldon's shoulders. He signalled with a jerk of his head for Eileen to shoo his two goggling children away. He had only intended to make report, show a bit of efficiency—or had he? The uncomfortable thought niggled that maybe he'd been seeking cover.

"Well done, Sergeant," Inspector Patrick said, smarmy swine. "Why are you telling me this?"

"Matters affecting community security, sir."

"Anything happened to him? Accident?"

"No, sir. He's not here yet."

There was no stopping this man in spate of sarcasm. "Is he running amok in your village allotments, Sergeant?"

"No, sir."

"Then carry on, Sergeant," Inspector Patrick instructed with maddening calm. "Protect the peace of the realm."

"Yes, sir."

"And, Sheldon. We heard about Taunton's verdict being quashed. We're on the telegraph route and everything down here in Colnebridge."

The receiver clicked, buzzed. The bastard, Sergeant Sheldon fumed. One day . . . He stamped out to the garden shed for his boots. The frigging patrol round the village could wait. He felt a desperate need to flail among the cabbages in his allotment across the way. He bawled furiously through the back door saying where he'd be for the next hour and marched across the road. He didn't even wait for his coffee, a sure sign of exasperation.

Eileen was playing finger houses with Mark and Bettina. She acknowledged his shout, recognizing the source of Joe's rage. That man Taunton they were all on about. She tried not to sigh. Joe was the compleat policeman. Even in rage his instinct ruled him. The gardening allotments were practically in the centre of the village, near the pond and the Queen's Head. Go over there at this time of day and you'd find every village gossip within reach.

Sarah Horn had to pass the doctor's surgery on her way to the village hall. "Having a well-earned rest, Dr. Salford is," she commented, nodding at the lighted surgery.

Her companion, Mrs. Jones, smiled, reassured at the sight of Clare's blonde head bent over her desk. "Finished surgery, more than like."

"Pretty as a picture," Mrs. Horn agreed. "Almost . . . framed there, isn't she? Like your Nathaniel's Easter tableau, for anyone to admire."

"Oh tush," Mrs. Jones deprecated. "She's young, but not that guileful."

"Do you not think so, Zuleika?"

"And popular. We're lucky to have somebody so conscientious. Especially these days."

"Will your Nathaniel be along tonight?"

"He's there now," Zuleika Jones informed her. "He's chairman."

"And very properly." Nathaniel Jones was the tempestuous and opinionated lay preacher at the Free Chapel, the only religious enterprise to rival Reverend Watson's established orthodoxy.

Mrs. Horn smiled disingenuously as they turned into the gravelled footpath towards the village hall. "I was so relieved he accepted the Guild's proposal to lead us."

"He sees it as his bounden duty."

"The only one as does, if you ask me," Sarah intoned righteously. "That Reverend's too stuck up. And it seems Dr. Salford's on the killer's side."

"Well . . ." Zuleika Jones was countering weakly as they approached the hall, when Sarah sensed the opportunity for a final barb.

"And I suppose you're right about Dr. Salford. We couldn't hope for somebody as clean-living as Dr. Chesterton anyway, could we?"

"Sarah! You can't mean that—"

But Mrs. Horn was already advancing on Mr. Downs, the longest-serving of the village's schoolteachers and making her way into the tiny hall where quite an assembly of the villagers was gathering with the social club members, lining up the folding chairs to face the stage. Mrs. Jones went slowly in after her friend.

A surgery without patients and the attendant hubbub is a cold place. Clare was glad to go through to her living area. For a while she tried to concentrate on a novel but her attention wandered and she put her book down, listening with half an ear for the phone. Once they all went an undoubted chill settled over the consulting-room, the corridor and Jackie's crammed alcove, while the waiting-room didn't bear looking at. Old John Chesterton, now retired to Frinton-on-Sea ten miles away and engaged in bitter struggles with local dahlia growers, had told her how essential it was to keep work separate from self. He'd gone on about this during her takeover period. "Wife and knife in different boxes, lass," he'd said time and again. "That's the reason the corridor door locks automatically." He had always chuckled there, adding: "The health committee thought how careful I was, thinking to protect drugs from marauders and visitors." Then he would stab a finger at the door. "Best friend a doctor can have. Shut out all the technology or you'll go mad, never have a life of your own."

He'd called it survival. This deliberate separation meant you survived, personality intact. Once lose that attitude and you dissolved in the vast technological empire that was modern medicine. You became a compulsive doctor, a hundred-percenter without a mind of your own. "Isn't that the idea?" she had asked, only partly teasing but consciously disturbed. It was a serious problem. The old doctor's cynical philosophy held a startling element of self-preservation. "Medicine is full time, John."

He had answered mildly, "Of course the *service* is. Or should be. But that doesn't mean you must be the sole provider of its continuity. Remember it's night and day. Every God-sent hour. Without an occasional break, your judgement vanishes."

"All jobs incur a risk of being too involved."

"Nonsense. Other jobs are about cars, bricks, pots and pans. Ours is people."

He had gone on to explain his safety-valve. "It's Dr. Greig over in Fieldham. Too young, like you," old Chesterton had twinkled, "and in a permanent diagnostic rush, but reliable. We've done two nights on, two off, for the past eighteen months."

Clare inherited the arrangement. Tonight was Andy Greig's

first night of his two, thank heaven. She had phoned him with the usual messages about the "state of play" as he liked to call it. The mongol child at the Westons, now two and chesty as ever, despite putting Esther Batsford on to its physiotherapy. The perennial trouble with old Stan Deller, who always knew better than Nurse Batsford and everyone else about his insulin with the result that he'd slipped into hypoglycaemic coma twice since Christmas. Andy's practise at Fieldham was much less bother. This swap arrangement sometimes made Clare feel guilty because Andy often had a hell of a time with her surly Beckholtians. His lot were so much more co-operative, even friendly.

She thought about the television, decided no. Then looked across at the tray, sherry and white wine. The silver was a gift of Dr. Chesterton and had come complete with silver chained nameplates. Rather pretentious nowadays, and she'd had to hide the madeira one because it was no use having something you can't stand. ("One drink's a godsend, lass; two'll rescue you on bad days. Never a third, though.")

The electric fire flickered its imitation flames. Cleaner, but less satisfying than a real coal fire. Perhaps it was nostalgia, or maybe even a desire to return to the primitive. Like the village seemed to be doing now, under the threat of Les Taunton's return. She shut the book, gazing at the painted coals. What had he been like? Jackie Hughes told her he'd been nice, a "bit wet" and often dreamy. He'd done a nice job on his cottage, which stood on the other side of the narrow farm lane from old Deller's, doing the thatching and restoring the windows. "My man passed him some cabbage sets last autumn," Jackie informed her during a slack time after surgery had closed. "He left some shallots in return." Then Jackie had paused and shivered. "When I was alone at the house. Never thought anything of it then, of course. But now . . ."

But now there's this primitive fear the whole village feels. Even now the extremists would be at the hall yapping their silly heads off. If the law says this Les Taunton's innocent, Clare lectured to herself, then he is and should be treated as such. She heard voices in the road, probably on their way to the hall. She waited until they were no longer audible, and got up to draw the curtains.

For some reason she felt restless, ill at ease with herself and the village. That bitter little passage-of-arms with La Horn must have disturbed her more than she realized. She went into the study. One more minute's indecision and she lifted the receiver to phone Ken at the police station. She could always pretend it was about Taunton. She had to get out of the village for the evening.

"Inspector Young, please."

CHAPTER 5

The hall was thick with cigarette smoke. Nathaniel Jones had been holding the floor now for an hour despite Eric Carnforth's despairing signals to George Falconer. And people were shifting in their hard seats—always a bad sign, which anybody who had helped to run the village pantomimes could recognize. Nathaniel surged on, clutching his lapels and throwing his head back. Bloody latter-day Gladstone, George groaned to himself.

A good third of the adult population of the village had turned up, even if the doctor and the priest had stayed away. Joe Sheldon was here, though standing impartially in uniform by the exit. George ran his eye round the assembly. On most occasions women outnumbered the men. Tonight they were about equal, but maybe the proximity of the social club next door was one excuse.

"This man," Nathaniel Jones was coursing on, "this wretched man was ac-tu-all-y employed in this village. He worked here. Among us. Among our children. Every single day. And—" he held up a warning hand—"and every single *night*."

A murmur ran round the hall. George's attention returned

quickly, having wandered to thinking about the paint flaking off the ceiling near the tiny stage. Time they got that done again or there'd be hell to pay when some little dancer got her dress soiled. They always went for the cheapest paint.

"Can we tolerate this criminal's return?" Nathaniel was starting his thunder, making his voice boom like when doing his hellfire bit in the chapel. "Are we going to remain som-no-lent while this criminal walks among us again?"

He paused for fullest effect. There was a good deal of head-shaking going on, with Mrs. Horn calling a loud "No!" and looking round for support. "Then here's what we do, people of Beckholt!" Thumbs in his waistcoat pockets now, George noticed sardonically. Joe Sheldon seemed unhappy, but these things always blew over. Only natural for a copper, but when he'd lived in the village as long as I have he'll know that these arguments are only a storm in a teacup.

"We petition the authorities!" Nathaniel boomed, his sonorous voice echoing down the hall.

"I second that!" Sarah Horn cried. Her cheeks were red spots, bright discs above her scrawny neck and her spectacles gleaming with an unfair share of the hall's meagre strip lighting.

"Agreed!" a few voices called. George was mildly surprised. Beckholtians were not usually so reactive.

"I call for volunteers to carry the petitions round this village!"

"The Guild of Village Wives volunteers!" Sarah Horn called, standing.

"We'll ask our members," Eric Carnforth nodded.

"I want names now," Nathaniel corrected him severely. "Is the Men's Confraternity found wanting? I call for volunteers!"

People rose and stretched thankfully. Others leaned through the press and spoke to Mrs. Horn who had found a pencil and paper from somewhere and was busily taking details. Zuleika Jones was passing names along. George rose and rubbed his buttocks surreptitiously. The atmosphere lightened. He found himself near the new teacher.

"Not volunteering, Ed?"

"I think not, George. You?"

George grinned, loading his pipe. "Too old." He lowered his voice as people began chatting and moving towards the exit. "One thing I've learned in this village, Ed. Never take sides. You never go wrong that way." For a second time George was mildly surprised that evening. Ed Edgeworth did not smile. In fact the young schoolteacher seemed decidedly worried. "What's the matter, Ed? Kids playing up?"

"No. They're fine. It's . . . it's this meeting."

George gave a few passing greetings to villagers as they left and stood with the teacher on the gravel. It was dark now, coming on to rain. A night wind had sprung up, shushing its way through the trees around the village. He crouched expertly, lighting his pipe. "No chance to get a word in sideways on, eh?" He chuckled, shaking his head. "Old Nathaniel'll bust a gut one of these days, gabby old sod."

"It's not that." Ed scuffed the gravel with his shoe. "It's wrong. Vigilante stuff, like in the Westerns."

George laughed aloud. Several departing people grinned good nights at them both.

"You've seen too many films. This is Beckholt."

"We've no right, George. Raising this petition, holding meetings as if we're bent on driving this chap away."

"Isn't that the idea?"

"It's against the law, though. That's the point I'm making."

"But Joe Sheldon said nothing."

"Maybe he should have," Ed said soberly. "Maybe I should have."

George suddenly called: "Here, Joe. A minute."

Sergeant Sheldon emerged from the porch and crossed over to them. "Got a licence for that pipe of yours, George?"

George guffawed. "They wouldn't give me one. Young Ed here's worried about the meeting. Thinks maybe we did wrong holding it. Nothing illegal in it, were there?"

The policeman shrugged. "Don't think so. As long as it's peaceful I don't mind."

"Pretty boring, if you ask me."

"It's wrong," Ed insisted, conscious he'd lost the argument by the opposition's default. Now the hall was emptying the atmosphere was diluted and the village felt normal again. "It's as if we were . . . well, making threats."

"A petition's allowed," Sheldon said.

"I know. But to which authority? And we never settled what the petition was going to say."

"Why," George put in, "suggesting that Les Taunton be . . ." he paused, thinking.

"Go on, George," Ed prompted gently. "That the man be . . . what? Expelled? Sent packing? *Made* to leave?"

"No. Nothing like that, I'm sure," George said uncomfortably.

"I just asked Mr. Jones that," Sheldon said. "It's to advise Taunton of the village's feeling."

"Won't he sense that the moment he's back?" Ed demanded.

"Well, this would make it . . . more pointed."

"Then it's not a petition, is it?" Ed waited for an answer but neither of the men spoke. "It's a statement, not a request. You can say no to a request. But a pointed statement is the first part of an argument. And arguments lead to a scrap."

"Not in this village, they don't," Sheldon snapped.

George stepped closer to them, frankly worried now by heightening emotions. The meeting seemed to have left a bad taste in everybody's mouth. "It'll blow over. You'll see." He fumbled for another match. His damned pipe had gone out again. "In this village it always does."

"Let's hope so," Ed said. He tried to smile at Joe Sheldon.

Joe gave him as affable a nod as he could manage in the circumstances. "Maybe it already has," he said. "Unpalatable things have a way of being forgotten here."

George remembered the flaking paint again. "And even if they're not," he capped, giving them all something innocuous to chuckle at. They moved off into the darkness.

CHAPTER 6

Clare tasted the wine, replaced it by the bedside. Ken smiled at her grimace.

"It's good for you, Doctor."

She raised her hair and flopped back on the pillow. "I wish you wouldn't call me that. Not here."

"Sorry. What's the matter?" He put his arm round her and together they lay looking at the shadows on the ceiling. "I did exactly as you instructed. Came at your bidding."

"I know. It's that bloody village."

"Don't let it get you down, Clare."

"Normally I don't."

"So what's abnormal all of a sudden?"

"Oh, nothing."

Ken smiled, but she was puzzling him. When the chance had come to move near where he was stationed they had both been jubilant, even if it was into a small village in East Anglia which seemed miles from anywhere. And sooner or later they would be able to stop this farce and live together properly.

"We're all right, aren't we, Clare?"

"Of course," she answered, but her voice was listless. "Nothing like that."

"People said anything?"

"About us? No. If they suspect they keep it to themselves."

Ken chuckled. "That means we're safe. You're just tired after too many night calls. And after seducing me like you did."

Clare smiled. "Was I so obvious?"

"Worse. Demanding. Though why I should sympathize with you when I've had such a hell of a day, God knows."

Clare ran her hands over his flanks as he spoke. Overweight, if anything, and definitely ill-groomed, no matter how much police training he'd had. Ken felt her fingers wander, and held her breast firmly. It was a curious fact, but her interest in his flesh puzzled him every time they met at the cottage. You'd think a doctor was somehow above it all.

"How can an inspector have a hard day?" Clare asked idly. "You're boss. Word is law and all that."

"Trouble with Patrick."

"Inspector?" She'd heard his name often enough from Ken. "Uniformed branch?"

He nodded. "Silly man. There's a chap coming out today . . ." He raised himself on his elbow suddenly, looking into her face. "Taunton. From Beckholt. Your village."

"Don't remind me."

"Your policeman phoned in. Patrick ballocked him off the line, came grumbling to me about whining local stations. I rocketed him for not taking enough details."

"Don't let's talk about it." Clare listened to the wind. It was a sea wind blowing in gusts up the estuary and roughing the valley woods. Rain was starting, tapping erratically at the windows. That meant the drive home would be difficult. The road from Goldhanger wound through so many small woods.

"Is there a lot of feeling?" Ken persisted.

"In the village? Of course." Clare sat up irritably, though the cold struck instantly at her shoulders and she had to reach out for her cardigan. She pushed Ken's hand away.

"That's unfair," he protested. "Flaunting yourself, then the sailor's elbow."

"There's one wicked old bitch in particular," Clare grumbled, taking up her wine. "Raising a petition."

Ken groaned. "As long as it doesn't come to us. Who's it for?"

"They don't even know themselves. Wanted me to go to some meeting. And the priest. And the sergeant."

"That serious? No wonder Sheldon rang in."

"Ken." Clare turned to look down at him, taking his hand again as a peacemaking gesture. "What can they do?"

"To Taunton? Nothing."

"I mean, they can't stop him working, anything like that?"

"No. He's free as a bird."

"And he lives in the village. They can't deprive him of his own home. Surely there are laws—"

Ken lifted himself up, grunting, and leaned on Clare's bare shoulder. "Correct. Unless he rents the place. And even then it takes months, even years, to recover a rented dwelling from a tenant. No. He's safe."

"They sounded so . . . so self-righteous," Clare explained. "If they'd come just saying they were worried—well—that would have been different. But they made my blood boil."

"The trouble is they think he did it. Everybody does."

"Then why was he let off?"

"Appeal." Ken snorted with derision. "Bloody clever lawyers," he grumbled against her neck. He was feeling sleepy "He's guilty as hell to me."

Clare nudged him awake. "He can't be guilty and innocent. Evidence is evidence, or it doesn't exist. Like in science."

Ken rubbed his face to waken sufficiently to argue back and reached for his own glass across Clare.

"Science? Don't make me laugh, love. Science is methodical. It's logic. There's none of that in Law. Once you're in a court you're in a jungle. It's trial by battle. Logic doesn't come into war."

Clare moved his hand from her thighs. "You mean he could still be guilty, and free?"

"It's happened."

"You sound . . . guarded. And the converse could be true— that he could just as easily still be in gaol and be innocent?"

"That's happened too. Look, love—"

"But judges just don't throw a verdict—a *murder* verdict—out on appeal unless the prosecution is hopeless, do they? They can't."

"That old chap, whatsisname, lived across the road from Taunton . . ."

"Deller?"

"Deller. He's diabetic. Maybe gaga most of the time. His evidence was always doubtful. But everybody believes it. The jury did." Ken gazed at Clare almost belligerently. "And me. I believed it, too."

"That Taunton was sitting alone in his cottage? Nothing wrong in that. Lots of people—"

"For three hours? In the dark? Late evening?" Ken nodded. "The man's almost illiterate, never gets books from the library van when it calls. It's practically all he can do to read the race card in a newspaper. He didn't have the television on—people pass occasionally and nobody saw the flicker of his set. Remember it can be seen through the window from the lane."

"Maybe he wanted to sit in the dusk." Clare raised her head defiantly at his incredulous laughter. "People do. What's wrong with that? It's his own cottage."

"Dusk falls like a stone here near the coast." Ken was uncomfortably aware that they were no longer tired lovers comfortably pillow-talking. "People *can* do all sorts of things in their own cottages. But it's what they *usually* do that counts."

"Maybe he felt unwell."

"And maybe he killed that girl," Ken said doggedly. "She was found beside the hedge, sixty feet from his garden."

"Three footpaths come together there," Clare shot back. "All sorts of folk might use them."

Ken tried to keep his voice gentle. "But *usually* they don't. That's the sort of logic the law uses, reasoning from the habits of people."

"You mean we're not to know the truth, not even yet?"

"That's right, love. If old Deller hadn't been a diabetic, Taunton would be up the river for life."

"Is that the only reason?"

"You can't blame the law, not this time." Ken indicated his empty glass and Clare poured from the cold bottle. "Doc Chesterton testified old Deller was well—but only fairly well, as old elderly diabetics go. The old man could have nodded off, been distracted, had to go to the loo, anything. And he's a great radio fiend."

"He said he was watching all the time. How horrid."

"Give it up, love. People'll believe Taunton's a killer till the day he dies."

"There's one thing, Ken." Clare sounded calm for the first time that evening. "If Taunton's truly innocent, the real murderer's free. Outside."

"Yes, love. And probably been living among Beckholtians since before you arrived in the village." Ken put the glass down and pulled her beneath the sheet with him. "No good worrying about things like that."

She smiled at him, their faces touching. "Sorry. Nearly a row, wasn't it?"

"But not quite."

She came against him and twined her leg over his body. "Thanks, Ken," she said. "You're a real help."

As they began to doze, she was thinking—not like the rest of them in that useless village. And as for that priest, how stupid can a man actually be?

Ken felt his own sleepiness dwindle as Clare slipped away into silence and regular breathing. His mind worried at her account as a butcher's dog worries at a bone, mechanically and without enthusiasm because there were plenty more where that came from, but unable to leave it alone because what else were bones for?

Clare was his lifeline. For all she was a doctor, she represented a window into normality for him which made her doubly —no, trebly—essential. For sex, for a promise of a stable future with a bright humourous woman, and now for that priceless insight into the dour rural world in which they lived. And of course she sensed it. She knew he was hers, that he belonged. Had done since that first day, in fact, when she had called with details of a suicide case. There had been no pause, no sense of interrogation, no doubt about his creaking marriage or about the part Clare was to play in his life.

Poets had it all wrong. The woman was the owner, the man the possession. He had no choice. She had all the choice in the world.

But this priest recurred and recurred in her conversation. He looked at her sleeping face on his shoulder and brushed her hair away from her closed eyes with his free hand, as if to help her to see. No matter what happened to Les Taunton, he suddenly knew that, for the first time since they had met, he would need all his vigilance.

Even dogs fought to stay owned.

CHAPTER 7

Jenny Tree could suss the mood of her public bar with her eyes shut. So she said. And especially tonight, when even a stranger would sense the aggro seething below the surface. Not too far below, either.

The Queen's Head was heaving, having filled up late. That was a clear danger signal. A shoddy little place, albeit right in the centre of the village, the pub had never been all that popular, especially among incomers. The other two taverns collared most of the trade, the poor Queen's Head being left with the artisans, a cluster of noisy farm workers who still weren't ashamed of their ancient mode of speech. This pub gave safe space to such—a refuge.

"Never seen so many, Jenny." Her husband Del faced the optics as he pressed a glass upwards for gin.

"You're right." Jenny sensed his worry but kept her expression cheerful. Del flicked a tonic cap odd, spun back for another spirit.

"Mick Robie's about."

"Oh, Christ."

They might have been exchanging a quick joke. Jenny's apprehension grew. If Del was anxious enough to use the old taverner's trick of loading unrequired drinks at the spirit optics to pass her a word or two without customers overhearing, well, something was badly wrong.

"Jenny! Letting us croak o'thirst?"

"Wait your turn, Ned Harris!"

"*Been* waitin'!"

Jenny heaved on the bitter peg. Soon the new beer dispensers would make serving twice as fast and much easier, though naturally this lot would grumble like mad.

"That bad?" Jenny cracked back.

Ned Harris leered across the bar at her, all scagged brown teeth. A grubby little man, he laboured for Fogg Powell on the biggest village farm. Supposed to be a wonder tractor man.

"Mick Robie," Ned said proudly. "One's his."

"We're honoured. He's usually up at the White Hart."

"He came over for the meeting."

The hubbub stilled a moment, then swelled again as the door latch went. Mick Robie entered, big in corduroys with a gipsy-style leather waistcoat. Jenny smiled with the rest as a chorus of shouted welcome rose.

"Shut that bleedin' thing off for a start!"

Del nodded at Jenny's swift side glance. She pulled the plug on the juke-box which trailed to a growling halt and caused more laughter.

"Thank Gawd."

"Your tottle, Mick," from Ned.

Mick was at the bar, heaving his glass up without even a nod to Ned, who was almost grovelling. The shove-ha'penny game had packed in the instant Mick arrived. A group of eight or nine of the lads were standing talking desultorily, their game partly done. More ready for trouble there. Jenny saw thankfully that the darts players were going on and on, obsessional as ever, ignoring the centring of attention on Mick.

"Rubbidge talk up a' there," Mick pronounced loudly.

"Sorted out yon looby Taunton?" asked Bob Barber, goal keeper on the village team.

"Nar, not them." Mick drained the glass and slammed it on the bar. "Talk, talk."

"'Nuther tottle for this un," Bob called to Jenny.

All eyes were on Mick as he turned to lean elbows on the bar. Jenny pulled the pint, feeling the man's magnetism, the violence which radiated from him. Uncouth and boisterous, he seemed to rule everyone in his immediate vicinity.

"What Taunton needs is two-sticks," Mick pronounced.

"Ar. Sort him out."

Bob passed Mick his fresh pint. Del was trying to talk up old Vincent, the one-pint-a-night violin maker, but it was a forlorn hope of easing the tension. Mick's mention of the flail was ominous.

"Get rid on him, that's what's needed."

"Mick's right."

"Bet he's been home since mucklight. And Olive Hanwell buried a furlong off."

Del was signalling to Jenny, his hand below the bar level, but definitely swivelling at the wrist as if about to raise it to his temple as a salute. The ubiquitous sign for authority. She was to phone Sergeant Sheldon now.

"I'll need no help," Mick was bellowing. "But them as want can come."

The youths were grinning, nodding. Bob Barber was finishing his drink fast.

"Let's go, lads."

Jenny hadn't moved though Del would know she had definitely recognized his signal. She smiled with determination as Mick faced her to set about his pint. "I hope you lads aren't heading for trouble, Mick Robie."

"Always have been," he cracked into the responsive laugh. "Why change now?" He leaned forward confidentially, lifting his eyebrows at the view of her plump cleavage. "Anyway we can't have our village maidens mauled by the like of Taunton." He grinned at her, the wave of sweat and leather for an instant shocking her with its overpowering maleness and the reek of potential violence. "We want them left for us. And I mean you for me."

Jenny's attempted cool weakened. "Then you be careful."

"Worrit I'll get a tannin'?"

A few of the lads shouted to Del that Mick Robie was chat-

ting his missus up. Del grinned and made some coarse remark.
Jenny served an old gaffer in the corner as the lads swarmed out
after Mick, then quickly went through to the back parlour and
dialled Joe Sheldon's number.

Les Taunton was surprised to find his electricity cut off. His
place never did have gas. Until he started buying the thatched
cottage on a mortgage which he couldn't understand, the only
means of light had been lanterns and candles. Plenty of wood
for fires, and anyway he read little—"I'm no scholar," was his
defence.

His journey had been uneventful. Train to Colnebridge, then
a long walk along the flyover road, cutting off through the fields
past Ford Farm where Mr. Henriques's lovely Jersey cows went
round on a kind of carousel, eating and being milked by chug-
ging coughing tubes while the bloody cowman did nothing but
stand gawping. Then splash across the ford, and through the
darkness up along the valley shoulder to where the footpath
turned into a proper metalled lane. A single old-fashioned street
lamp, newly converted to electricity, shone its household bulb
weakly into the lane. A few of the bungalows and cottages
among the hedges showed lights and made the going easier, but
he knew the village like his own hand. Old Mr. Deller's telly
was flickering across the narrow lane, and Mrs. Winner's outside porch light was on.

God, the cottage garden was overgrown. It came on to rain as
he waded chest-high through the impossible sea of weeds. He
was drenched when he finally unlocked the front door, getting
himself soaked under the pouring thatch. Maybe he should
change it to slate and gutters, like so many folk had in these
parts.

He stepped inside, suddenly almost in tears at the familiar
aroma of cottage plus—well—plus himself. He put the case
down and felt round for a match. Then he smiled to himself.
Hawkeyes, his cat. He'd bought a tin of catfood for her. Mrs.
Winner would have looked after her really well. And he'd
promised to come straight round for Hawkeyes the minute he
got back.

He left his case there and the door open and retraced his path to the lane. Mrs. Winner was only the other side of his hedge, same side of the lane. He walked round, coming into the lamplight and smiling towards old Stan Deller's flickering telly. The old man spent hours each night glued to his screen, more as an excuse to be positioned for seeing who passed along the lane than to enjoy the programmes. And radio all day long.

The neatness of Mrs. Winner's garden was a village legend. Several times a month she'd complained about the blessed hedge, but a man had to go out to work as well as trim his garden. A woman alone has nothing to do all day long but bustle among her greenery. And he never seemed to have as many hours to the twenty-four as other folk.

He knocked. Wisely Mrs. Winner had got old Foster to tile her roof, red pantiles instead of thatch. Town folk were always coming through and saying how sad it was to see the good old ways go, but they avoided them and lived in the most comfortable way they could find. Shrewd townies. The latch went, and Mrs. Winner stood framed in the doorway. She gave a gasp, stepped back still holding the latch.

Les smiled, taking a pace into the narrow porch. "Hello, Mrs. Winner." He felt quite shy. "I'm home." Why did she look so pale?

She had a hand at her throat.

"I come round, then," he began to explain, but she emitted a faint breath and slammed the door on him.

"Go away!" she shouted. "Don't you come here!"

Puzzled he put his face to the door. New paint, he noticed foolishly in the porch light. "Mrs. Winner? It's me. Les."

She sounded hysterical. "I'll call Sergeant Sheldon! I will!"

"I come for Hawkeyes," he explained. "Please."

"Go away! Go away!"

He shrugged. Women had these tantrums. Everybody knew that. Though when he'd first settled in she'd been round his cottage every minute of the day, it seemed, wanting to do this and that and clearing up so you couldn't find anything. He shrugged and went round to his own place. Hawkeyes would have to wait until tomorrow, that was all. No good worrying about Hilda Winner. Maybe she wanted to keep Hawkeyes? But Hawkeyes would come home, of that Les was absolutely sure.

In the dark cottage he savoured the familiar aroma. Odd how all living things gave out scents, marks, sweat, as if to dab their own imprints on a small part of the world, and so indelibly establish one fragment as a kind of private empire.

He was about to strike a match, having found a candle stub on the door lintel, when the noises began. People? At this time of night?

Puzzled, he moved back to the open door. Some of the lads, laughing and shouting to each other. Half-smiling at some of the recognizable voices and their homely dialect abuses, he stood in the opening to greet them. Mick Robie's voice. Bob Barber. Terry Gepp from the garages, Frank the big fullback. Les had drawn breath to shout a greeting when their words struck him.

"The bastard's not home!"

"Maybe the frigging murderer's hiding!"

They'd stopped. He could see them in the oblique light from the lane's lamp. He pressed back in the doorway, carefully pulling the door to without noise and shooting the bolt. His hands felt damp, his neck cold. They weren't after him, surely. Maybe it was some joke?

"He'll be along. Any minute."

"For a postlin'."

A thrashing? Him? Les, their friend? Laughter. He jumped, frightened, as the window beside the door crashed in, the pane disintegrating. A sliver sliced the skin on his right hand. Glass was everywhere. Another stone thudded against the door. They were coming closer.

"We'll wait inside, lads." Mick was calm, belligerent.

"Hap' he's a drink hidden!"

Then he heard the distant shout.

"Shush, lads." Mick was at the door, a yard or so away. "Yes, Mr. Deller?"

Les chilled. Old Stan Deller had been watching, seen him arrive, probably watched him in the light of Mrs. Winner's porch.

He crunched as softly as he could through the little vestibule, past his bedroom and into the kitchen. They were bound to have had a drink or two. And the front door would give easily under any pressure. It was no place to stay. That was as far as he could think.

"He's in there, lads!" Old Deller's voice carried reedily through the night air. "Just now. I seed him!"

"Inside? Sure?"

"This minute. With his case. Went round bothering Mrs. Winner. She locked him out! You ask her."

"The bastard!"

"Right!" Mick was instantly issuing orders, demonic in his enthusiasm.

Stones crashed through windows. One skittered along the corridor and came to rest against his foot where he waited trembling at the kitchen door. He'd never had a key for this and for several ugly moments he struggled shakily to draw the bolts from top and bottom. They'd rusted slightly and both squeaked as he managed to pull them aside. The metal door handle was full of noise, but the lads were now battering at the front door, a terrible racket. His breath was choking him, almost sobbing in his throat. Why were the lads doing this? What did they want him for? The night air washed over his face, for some reason warmer than that inside his cottage despite the falling rain.

They were shouting with jubilation. The front door was caving in, splintering under the battering. No lack of big round flintstones in these parts. The only way into the cottage was from the lane. Otherwise it had to be the fearsome hedge. He was breathing like a runner, steaming from his panic heat and rainsoaked clothes.

"Round the back, lads. Bob and Frank!"

They were coming. He stepped out, pulled the kitchen door to behind himself and waded through the weeds in a straight line. His two Bramley apple trees were mercifully low hanging —another testimony to his gardening indolence. He stood behind the nearer one, shivering, sweat pouring down his face and starting his eyes stinging. Senselessly they started bashing at the back door, little realizing it was unlocked. More glass

went. Something splintered. There were shouts from round the
front. How many were there? Maybe ten or a dozen at first.
Now there seemed scores. And it would only be a few seconds
more before they beat their way in and realized he was hiding
close by. The little glim from Hilda Winner's porch light and
the distant glow of the lane's lamp, once friendly, were now en-
emies.

A crash. The back and front doors went simultaneously, judg-
ing by the howls that went up.

"Bugger's in there somewhere!"

"Make sure he doesn't get past, lads!"

Now.

He ran low and fast across the garden, frantically parting the
tall weeds as he went, the way racing swimmers breast water.
The hedge loomed, scratched at his face and hands. Sloe
blackthorn was worse even than the suppler hawthorn with its
longer twigs. He struck blindly forward and upwards, eyes closed,
clawing his way into the hedge with blood starting from palms,
fingers, face and knees as the thorns impaled him. He did not
understand. Nobody in his right mind risked a hedge, yet here
he was having to climb into the wild thing because his own people were after him.

The thorns impaled him again and again and again as he
scrabbled towards safety in the darkness.

CHAPTER 8

"Hello? Mrs. Sheldon? Can I speak to Joe, please. Urgently."

"Who's speaking?"

"Sorry. Shaw Watson. Sorry it's so late."

"Oh, Reverend. Joe's been called out. Some sort of trouble down near the Queen's Head."

Shaw dithered for a moment. He could see the slumped form of Les Taunton in the living-room from the hall. It was too serious to wait.

"Look." He tried for firmness, some decision. If only Eileen Sheldon hadn't been so quick to title him like that he would have reacted better. Now his spirits sank, weighted down by the cloth of his calling and all the ridiculous pomp that a laywoman's superstitious awe entailed. "Er—look. Is there another policeman anywhere?"

It sounded lame even to himself.

"Well, there's another at Fieldham, Reverend." The village was a few miles away and a policeman from there would take maybe an hour to find his way round the straggled houses in the dark. Eileen's voice was guarded. "And the Central. Wouldn't it be better to wait for Joe?"

She had made her point. Phoning Central implied a village policeman's inadequacy.

"This is very urgent," he said weakly.

"I'll tell you what, Reverend," Eileen said, anxious herself now. "The call came from Jenny Tree. Let me try to raise Joe at the pub."

"Only I suspect their bother's the same as I have here."

"Any message, then?"

He hesitated again. How pathetic he felt. "Well, could you please explain—*only* to Joe, though—that I've got Les Taunton?"

"At the vicarage?" She almost squealed her astonishment.

"Yes. He's rather the worse for wear. Maybe the doctor—"

Click. The dialling tone. She'd rung off. Please, he prayed to nobody in particular, please speak *only* to Joe. Once it got about . . . He dialled Clare Salford's duty number. A man answered.

"Dr. Greig here." A pause. "Yes?"

"Reverend Watson," Shaw answered helplessly. It was a night for titles. "Can I speak to Dr. Salford, please?"

"She's off duty, Reverend. Can I do anything?"

A decision came unbidden. "Thank you, but I particularly wanted her. A village matter."

"I quite understand. I'm afraid she has no private number."

"That's all right, Dr. Greig. I can pop across and leave her a note. It's not far."

"If you're sure . . . ?"

He returned to the living-room. Taunton was slumped back on the horsehair settee. His face was ravaged. Caked blood matted his hair. It's brown, the priest thought in surprise: dried blood caked on a man's lacerated face is brown. So those wonderful religious paintings of the last century are all utterly wrong. How awful. How truly terrible.

"Are you all right, Les?"

Taunton's eyes opened. "Yes, thanks, Reverend."

"You're in a mess. I'll get some water."

"I'll be okay."

He carried a towel and warm water through from the kitchen. The washing-up bowl was the only one he possessed, but surely there was nothing septic on plastic? He worried as he set the bowl on the floor.

"Can you take your jacket off, please?"

"I'll manage." Taunton struggled upright, groaning, to obey while the priest went to put more wood on the fire. The man's hands were a shredded mess. Even as he discarded his tweed jacket fresh blood started from his knuckles and the palms left bloodstains wherever they touched an object. Several thorns still protruded from his flesh.

"I'll clean it all up, Reverend," the man promised, worried about the blood.

"Stay still." Shaw clumsily started to wash the man's hands.

A trail of mud, leaves and grass led from the front door into the living-room where the priest had all but dragged the incoherent fugitive. Shaw's cassock was muddied from having caught the man as he slumped forward into the porch.

"I'll try to get some of those thorns out." Tweezers were the trouble. Not a pair in the house. He ran over the names of any women in Church Road who might fetch some. Perhaps not, on such a wild night, especially with Taunton as the beneficiary.

The poor man started groaning soon after the priest's crude surgery began. Blood stained the water to a bright pink. Too worried to reason now, Shaw dabbed ineffectually at Taunton's face—wasn't there something about care of eyes? Keeping an airway clear? Though the fugitive seemed conscious enough to manage most things himself.

"Here. Wrap your hands in the towel," he ordered hopelessly. "Keep them still. I'm going to bring the doctor."

"Reverend. They're after me."

Irritably Shaw removed the bowl and tried to cover the man's hands.

"Who?"

"Mick Robie, Bob Barber, Frank. A load on 'em."

"What for?" It sounded so unlikely.

"I dunno 'at, Reverend."

"Are you sure?"

"I seed 'em. Broke mi windows in. Smashed mi doors. I clumb through mi hedge to the field and run."

Shaw sat beside the shattered man. "Listen, Les. I'm going out—"

Alarm forced Taunton's eyes open. "Leave me here?"

"Listen. I can't do your hands and face properly. There are thorns everywhere. Your eyelids . . . it might be dangerous. If the villagers are after you, they'd hear an ambulance. I'll leave a note for Dr. Salford."

"You'll come straight back, Reverend?"

"I promise. But you must promise me something."

"Keep locked in?"

"That's it. I've phoned Joe Sheldon. Even if he comes, take no notice of his banging. *Don't open the door to anyone.* Understand? Not Joe, not police from town, not the doctor. Right?"

Taunton was half asleep from fatigue. His hands were only seeping now, and mercifully blood had ceased trickling down his temples. How much blood had the man lost, for heaven's sake?

He rose, got a mackintosh over his shoulders. Wellingtons and a plastic hood. An umbrella would be worse than useless out there. The wind had risen in the last half hour, and rain was driving on the gusting easterly against the rectory windows.

"Les? Can you hear me?"

"Mmmmh, Reverend."

"If," Shaw pronounced carefully, "if some people knock, and say it's urgent, can they come in and wait—what do you do?"

Les thought a moment. He had instructions. Reverend had given him instructions a few minutes back. His brain cleared wearily. "Don't let them in?" he suggested.

"Good. And listen, Les. If Sergeant Sheldon comes and orders you to open the door—what then?"

Les saw the priest's frown and said quickly, "Ask him to wait outside?"

"I've told you, Les. Mind, *nobody* must be let in."

"I'll keep the door locked, Reverend."

"I won't be long, Les. You just rest."

As he was moving to the door, Les called drowsily, "Reverend. This don't mean I'm to go back to court, do it?"

Shaw Watson paused at the door. "No, Les," he said. "This place is . . . is . . . *sanctuary*." He repeated the word, pleased and moved by the notion. "And nobody is allowed in a sanctuary. A special place."

"Like for birds?"

"Yes. Like for birds."

Shaw swung open the heavy door and stepped out into the storm.

CHAPTER 9

Ken halted his car in the turning circle of the surgery driveway.

"You could have stayed later."

Clare shrugged. "You—we—say that every time."

"Because it's true."

"We'd have to slog home sooner or later, no matter how long we postponed it." She eyed the dark outline of her house, the vague shifting darknesses of the huge foaming trees under press of the wind. It made her shiver. She drew her coat about her neck.

"Is that 'home'?" Ken asked.

"The surgery?" Clare thought a second. It was Dr. Chesterton's argument all over again. "Maybe the house is. I don't know."

"You mean no." Ken's tone was uncompromising.

"I mean I don't know," Clare replied, sharper than she intended, and could not prevent herself adding: "Is yours?"

"Yes. For the moment."

Clare turned to face him. "For the duration."

"What do I do, love?" Ken asked helplessly. "Enid's as uncontrollable as ever. You know about these mental things. I don't."

"I suppose you do what everybody else does, Ken." Clare's bitterness struck into him. The wisest thing would be to leave but his suspicion that he was more vulnerable than she made him want to argue it out. "Wait for events to make a decision for you."

"I'm not that facile."

"We all are." She opened the passenger door and put her arm round his neck leaning her face against his for a moment. "We see no easy way, dear. So we wait, hoping for the undergrowth to clear by a magic of its own. I'm the same, darling, in other situations. I do exactly that. We just mustn't delude ourselves."

"I don't, love. One day we'll—"

"One day your two children will be a year older. Then they'll be eleven and twelve. And fifteen. Then at the university. Then grown up. And Enid will still be sedated, but schizophrenic as ever." She drew away to find her handbag. "Patient doing as well as can be expected." Her voice was almost mocking. "Isn't that what we always say?"

"It's the children," Ken said helplessly.

"That's the spirit, darling." Clare gave him a smile in the car's interior light. "Let's truce it for now. Soldier on."

"You seem in a strange mood. Is it the Taunton business?"

Clare bussed his mouth quickly. "Let sleeping dogs lie." She shut the car door and ran through the rain towards her door. The glass weatherporch was a godsend, allowing her slight shelter while waving at Ken's departing car.

In the darkness on the opposite roadside, the priest watched the car pull out and turn downhill towards the main Colne-bridge road. He hadn't intended to spy on Dr. Salford and the man, but what could he do? In a way he was trapped between the urgency of his need for assistance and his own innate embarrassment at the situation. It needed nerve, he thought disgustedly—and you, Reverend Shaw Watson, have none. A born waverer. You stand here watching them in the downpour rather than do what any self-respecting man of decision would have done, namely coughed, scuffed noisily forward flashing your torch and giving them every chance to normalize their apparent relationship. But no. *Ditherer!*

He made himself count to a hundred from the time her door slammed before stepping clear of the hedge and trudging up to the door. His feet were soaked, trousers flapping wetly.

There were already lights on when he rang. She had shed her overcoat when the hall's brilliance silhouetted her. He faced up bravely feeling like a drowned rat.

"Er, Dr. Salford. I—I need your assistance, please."

"Why, Reverend." A slight hesitation, quickly concealed, he

noted with private bitterness. Decision seemed easy for a person of character. "Do come in. Isn't it a filthy night?"

"Terrible." He was immediately conscious of the pool forming from his plastic raincoat and hurriedly unfastened it. "I'd best not come in, Doctor. Flood you out."

She gestured him inside. "Is it yourself that's . . . ?"

"No, no." He realized she had shut the door and moved aside to avoid wetting her smart powder blue suit with his mackintosh. "Taunton."

"That man?"

"Yes. I phoned, but Dr. Greig answered. I—I hope it's all right? You being off duty."

"Perfectly."

"I thought perhaps to keep it in the village, you see. I left him at the vicarage."

"An accident?"

"Not really. Badly scratched and bleeding somewhat. A hedge, I believe."

He realized she was moving down the surgery corridor. The lights were on at the far end—her own dwelling. Was he expected to wait here? Was she going for her doctor's bag? He cleared his throat and spoke louder after her.

"Some bother." She did not pause. He raised his voice another decibel. "I gather there was some bother."

"He was conscious?" she asked over her shoulder.

"Er, yes. No permanent damage . . ." He felt stupid. How did he know whether there was permanent damage or not? He had come here because of his own profound ignorance.

"Do come."

She paused to release him from his anguish, turned and vanished into a room beyond the intersecting door. But what about his streaming mackintosh? And his squelching shoes?

"Er, coming," he called uncertainly. Had she sounded irritated? He often annoyed decisive people. He knew that.

He was now alone on the doormat, desperately seeking clues to do right in her place. Only minutes before he had seen her run through the rain, yet where was her own drenched overcoat, her headscarf? And doubtless her mother's splendid Afghan microweave carpet would be in ambush, waiting to be ruined forever by his clumsy flooding. In despair he slipped his mackintosh and let it crumple on the doormat and set off down the corridor. He knocked gingerly on the intervening door though it stood ajar, conscious of his wet trousers against his legs. That's the trouble with plastic raincoats, he was thinking when Clare appeared.

"I thought you'd got lost."

"Er—took my things off." He followed her into a comfortable well-lit room. Of course, he noted miserably, her own overcoat was flung casually over an upright chair by the wall. Probably not too wet. The car.

"No need. I come in all weathers. I take it Taunton has had a scare?"

"Some of the locals, I gather. Trying to break into his cottage. Bricks. That sort of thing."

"A fight? You said it wasn't too bad."

"He got away. Climbed through his hedge. Of course he's shaken, scared. Looks rather a mess."

"I'll come. Only be a second."

Their eyes held for a moment, the priest as uncertain as ever. The thought crossed Clare's mind that he had seen Ken leave, maybe even witnessed her with him. She saw his eyes waver and guessed that he had.

"Should I go on ahead?" he asked.

"No. It'll be quicker by car. Is he badly cut?"

"Not *cut* exactly."

Her mind went to instruments. She gestured an invitation to sit while she returned to the surgery. He did so, on the edge of the armchair. A feminine room, the emphasis on pastels and flowers, with mahoganies and rosewoods predominating. Decision showing again, he thought wryly. You either have it or you haven't.

In the surgery Clare was dog-tired. She had the emergency bag to hand, but picked up a battery of immunisations from the cold box of the fridge. Tetanus toxoid was a must. She felt vaguely cheated, probably weariness. And the infuriating hesitancy of that wretched priest. Like a terrier failing to fetch its stick from some canal and looking appropriately hangdog when facing the thrower.

She was unduly curt when, with another coat and headscarf, she collected him from her lounge. He squelched after her down the corridor to the surgery exit.

"I'll get the car. Please make sure you bang the door."

"Right."

Bloody man, she fumed inwardly, running for the garage. When he came slithering into the passenger seat she was ready for him. "Why did Taunton come to you, Reverend?" She slammed in gear.

"I don't know. Maybe he just blundered anywhere."

"Is he a churchgoer?"

"I heard he never used to be." The priest sounded apologetic about the fact. "I don't know about recently."

"He should have run to the police."

"Or the doctor."

"True." Clare realized too late he might have intended irony and caught at her temper.

They travelled in silence after that, but as the car slowed alongside the rectory gate the priest finished the conversation.

"I phoned Mrs. Sheldon for Joe to come. In case."

"In case of what?"

"I'm not sure."

She could not help herself snapping, "What *are* you sure of, Reverend?"

"Very little, Doctor."

Joe Sheldon was waiting inside his white panda car in the rectory drive. He emerged in his oilskin, his helmet badge picking up the beams from Clare's car.

"Fine night to be shut out, Shaw. Doctor."

"Good evening, Mr. Sheldon." Clare led the way.

"Somebody's inside but won't open up."

"Actually I told him not to," Shaw said. "Taunton."

"There was a right mob down his place not long since."

"He ran away."

"Did you see anybody following?" The policeman flashed his torch around the garden.

"I didn't look." Shaw took out his key and banged the knocker, calling loudly, "Les? Les?"

A shuffling sounded. "What?"

"It's me. Reverend Watson. I'm back. I'm going to come in. All right?"

The unlocked door refused to budge. A great deal of grunting went on before it swung open. Les was there, sheepishly trying to push the hall cupboard back in place against the wall.

"That's all right, Les. Leave it."

"I thought it best—in case," Les explained.

"You did very well. I've fetched Sergeant Sheldon and Dr. Salford to have a look at you."

"Jesus, Les!" Joe Sheldon took in Taunton's dishevelled appearance. "Dragged through a hedge?"

"Climbed through," Shaw answered for him.

"Sit down, please."

"Yes, Doctor."

"I'll be a few minutes," Clare told the two men.

Shaw Watson signalled with his eyebrows to Joe Sheldon. They left Clare and went into the small rectory study where a stale bottle of sherry was kept for emergencies.

CHAPTER 10

"Don't, Mick."

"Shut your prattlin', woman."

"I'll be rumpled. Del'll know—"

"Give it here." He tugged her left breast out of her blouse, making her gasp at the force of him.

Jenny was already dishevelled and breathless. Mick's thick hands seemed everywhere, and he refused to be still. Mick's man-smell was all Jenny could detect.

Del had gone upstairs when Jenny heard the scraping sound at the leaded glass. She'd wiped the bar down quickly and slipped out; leaving the latch down she would hear the rattle should Del recover sufficiently from his weariness to come searching for her. And, clever afterthought, she switched the light on in the downstairs toilet to allay suspicion.

"You bastard," she breathed, groaning as Mick's mouth leeched over her exposed nipple. "You only want me to tell lies for you."

He raised his head, breathing hard himself. "And why not, you bitch?" He pulled her hard against him, his thumbs crushing bruises in her thighs in sudden anger. "You phoned the Old Bill."

"I had to."

"You nigh got me caught." His hand cuffed her temple. "Only just caught sight of Joe's lights."

"*Bastard!*" Her head was ringing. Still the horrible animal's hands did not stop roaming, nor his belly ramming her against the outhouse's supporting beam. "But I told Joe you were out of the pub heading to the Colnebridge road."

"There's a clever girl. I'll give you a little present for that."

"I've . . . I'm not ready, Mick. It's a risk." She sensed his immediate anger and explained quickly, "You're usually away tonight."

He chuckled quietly, lifting her skirt. "Poor Frank and Bob got took." He was grinning, knowing the willingness of her.

"Your mates! You really are a—"

"Bastard?" His teeth fastened on her neck. She groaned and tried to pull away.

"Don't Mick. I mark easy. For Christ's sake . . ."

"Not easy enough for me," he breathed. "I see I'll have to work harder."

"What do you want me to say?"

"Tell Joe Sheldon I were in and out the taproom till you closed."

"He'll never believe me."

"Make him, stupid."

"How can I? He'll ask others."

"Just give that testimony. Promise."

"I promise, lovvie."

He was sucking at her and marking her legs with his great hands. She felt herself melting under his pressure. It was all so unfair. He could have any woman her age, and plenty younger too. He'd only come to protect himself, leaving his mates in the mire. They'd be too afraid of him, too loyal, to reveal the truth. And with her own testimony he'd be scot free. A swine, but she was unable to resist. She found herself helping him, breathing faster, slipping their garments and lodging her buttocks against the sacking which covered the barrels.

"Here, lovvie," she whispered. "Here I am."

He liked her hands to cup him for several moments before she parted for him. She knew that from the previous times. She worked him steadily and rhythmically, mouthing endearments.

"Now, Jenny."

Against all wisdom her eyes closed and all vigilance dissolved. Whatever trouble there'd be with Del, she knew in the last coherent moment her determination to protect the creator of this loving moment.

"Never fear, lovvie," she found herself crooning jerkily. "Never fear."

CHAPTER 11

The cleaning woman put her head round the consulting-room door. "'Morning, Doctor."

"'Morning, Mrs. Locking."

"Terrible trouble last night. That Taunton."

The charlady was delighted at this opportunity. The surgery was not due to start for nearly an hour and here was Dr. Salford already busy at her desk hurrying through those complicated case records.

Clare was cautious. She asked innocently, "Oh? He's back, I take it?"

Mrs. Locking leant on her broom confidentially. "Some of the men went over to his cottage. Fired it."

"*Fired* it?" Clare stopped leafing through the "T" file.

"Well, tried to. The rain stopped it. Did damage, though. He's over at the priest's house. Taking charity too far, if you ask me. Even for a priest."

"*Is* he dangerous, Mrs. Locking?"

"He killed poor Olive Hanwell, didn't he?" Mrs. Locking's indignation impelled her to action again, savagely raising a cloud of dust from the reception area.

"*Leave* that, please, Mrs. Locking. Do it tomorrow."

"Right, Doctor." The char went off for the vacuum-cleaner. "It's not over. You see. They'll have him, no matter what Joe Sheldon does."

"Have him?"

"Finish him, I mean. Like he did to Olive."

Clare called her back. "Mrs. Locking. Are you serious?"

"'Course. Stands to reason." She grinned a gappy grin. "You don't know these village lads like I do. We call 'em lads, but they be'em men. And men do terrible things, terrible things."

Clare glanced at the clock. Seven-thirty. Jackie Hughes would be here at eight, for an eight-fifteen start of the routine clinic. The day was more controllable since she made everybody accept an appointments system, though it was still far from popular. Luckily no emergencies had been notified by Andy. A brief chat about Reverend Watson's call of the previous night had settled that.

But Dr. Chesterton had kept meticulous records and one envelope she'd never properly consulted was that of Les Taunton. Everybody had assumed Chesterton's evidence was the final medical word. And, since the old man had delivered Les twenty-three years ago as well as supervising his growth, maybe it was. She had just found Taunton's manila record envelope when the phone rang. It was Ken at his most official.

"Hello. Is that Dr. Salford, Beckholt?"

"Speaking."

"Inspector Young here, Doctor. About last evening. I've just had a report from Sergeant Sheldon that a local disturbance took place in your village."

"Yes. I heard, Inspector."

"I'm ringing to ask if any injuries came to your notice, Doctor."

"None of great importance, Inspector. Some scratches to one man."

"Did you witness any part of the disturbances?"

"Not myself, no."

"Very well, Doctor." He sounded relieved. "Thank you. Apologies for interrupting your work."

"Not at all." She paused, swiftly working out a formula to convey her private message to him. "It was good of you to ring."

Smiling, she replaced the receiver and read Les Taunton's medical record.

The day was overcast, typical early autumn with blustering winds to remind folk of the previous rainy night. George Falconer was at his roadside stall early. Tricia from the post office gave him the usual jeer as she cycled past.

"You'll sell nuthin' i' this village, George!"

"Get on!" he yelled, delighted at her greeting. "I sells to the throughcomers. Them wi' money and grand motors."

"Then lend us a quid!"

"I'll lend you the back o' mi hand, lass."

"You're too far gone!"

His stall stood on the roadside at a gap he had cut in the hedge bordering his smallholding. Mary had insisted on a bungalow when they had first set up together. The wisdom of this had become increasingly obvious. With a simple side extension the bungalow was usable as a store centre for their produce, and another extension gave cold store facilities for perishables. That and the ample hanging space for herb drying made the smallholding as viable as any in the area. A well-ventilated outhouse was needed for soft fruits—and, George thought with a chuckle, the money for it.

Within an hour five or six cars stopped on the way to busy Colnebridge. And within that same hour George, pleasant and chatty to any passing villager whenever an opportunity arose, had gleaned the main events of the previous night, and could guess more accurately now what feelings existed concerning Les Taunton. Mary fetched him out a cup of coffee at nine.

"Ta, love," he told her, as always. "I'll have elevenses at ten o'clock as well."

"Today will warm up, George."

He eyed the sky, nodded wisely. "More ways than one, I'm thinking."

"Taunton?"

"At the priest's house. The lads did Taunton's house over in the dark hours." He narrated the story.

"Eric Carnforth's been on the phone about that petition."

"I thought Sarah Horn wouldn't let it drop."

"Three hundred signatures, nigh on."

"Dear God! They must have been knocking on doors half the night."

"He wants to know when will he see you, decide on things."

"I don't like this, old girl," George said glumly. He adjusted his face to its usual good cheer and waved to an approaching car. The driver, a Fieldham man, had his order written out by a careful wife and was able to pull away without having stopped at all. "Like a bloody race track," George grumbled. "Barely time to say good day."

"Changing times, George," Mary commiserated, knowing his early stall time was the high spot of his day. "What'll I tell Eric?"

"Say I'll walk up to the White Hart about noon."

"All them pea-pickers?"

The incoming casual labourers, wanderers from one area of East Anglia to another as harvests and crops fell due, were unpopular. Locals usually avoided places they frequented. It was not uncommon to see notices outside village pubs: *No Pickers*

Served Here. The White Hart was the only one of the three taverns not to proscribe them—a profitable move during late summer, but one which caused the locals to transfer to other taverns.

"What you up to, George Falconer?" Mary asked.

"Nothing, lass. Just want no ears lissenin'."

Mary went in to do the decanting. Her next batch of homemade wine was due. Normally a job which interested and pleased her, today it held little attraction. Something in the village was wrong, badly wrong, when her outgoing George resorted to subterfuge. It wasn't like him.

Stan Deller offered the doctor a cup of tea, knowing she would scold him for trying to use her routine visit as a means of stealing a few extra calories.

"Don't think I don't know what you're up to, Stan."

"What's wrong with tea?" he demanded, pretending amazement.

"You'll blame me when your blood sugar goes up. And don't wag your finger at me."

"No patient is more obedient."

"Or craftier."

He eyed the ophthalmoscope with alarm. "What now?"

"Your eyes. Look at the corner."

"You looked at them last week. There something wrong?"

"If I look, then I'll know. Now the other corner." Clare straightened up after a few moments, letting out her breath. "Good as ever." She started folding her instruments away.

"Anything the matter, Doctor?" The elderly man was apprehensive at her renewed interest. "You usually leave my blood pressure to Nurse Batsford. Here. That's my television chair."

"Don't be so irascible. My word." She twitched the curtain aside. "Haven't you got a lovely view from here? Right across the lane to Mrs. Winner's and that old derelict place next to it . . ."

The old man chuckled, nodding. "Derelict? No, but it should be."

Clare pretended surprise. "Why do you say *should*? It looks

awful. Broken windows, thatch burned at that corner. Surely
nobody lives there?"

"Taunton. The killer."

Clare gasped. "*He* lives there? The man they let out yesterday?"

"He does. For the while."

"Is he leaving?"

"Not today. Tomorrow night he'll definitely be gone."

Clare let the curtain fall into place. "You're not suggesting
somebody will attack him?"

"Not while he's over at the priest's they won't. Don't know
about afterwards."

"Tell me, Stan."

"Nothing to do with me, Doctor." The old man's face closed
imperturbably. "I'm just a poor old diabetic who can't get
about like he used to. And that Nurse Batsford," he added spitefully, "Makes me do my own insulin injections."

"On my orders." Clare rose coolly and picked up her case and
folder of notes. "Have you any criticisms?"

"No, Doctor," he said meekly.

"See you on Monday, then. Nurse will pay her usual visits."

She said her goodbye and walked down his garden path, surreptitiously inspecting the lane. From where she had sat, by the
neat expedient of usurping the old man's favourite chair, there
was a good view of Les Taunton's cottage, including its hedge
opening into the lane. But from there the gated entrance into
Mrs. Winner's adjoining garden was concealed by Mr. Deller's
own hedge. The visit to Mr. Deller had not contributed much,
but the meagre facts were definitely news to her.

The rectory's visitor had proved unexpectedly resourceful, cooking tomatoes, boiling eggs and frying bread for breakfast after
attending Communion as the only congregant for that dawn.

"What will you do, Les?"

"Dunno, Reverend."

Nothing unusual in having only one member of the village
praying in the service, Shaw persuaded himself. A farming community naturally swapped devotions for harvest duties only too

readily at this time of year. Taunton was at once diffident and eager to be of use. They breakfasted together, rather uneasily on Shaw's part.

"You had a job in the garage before—er—before?"

"Yes. I ull go round there today. See about my job."

Shaw stirred his tea, thinking quickly. "Will he be open today?"

"Allus, by this time."

"Ah. Look, Les. Couldn't you postpone—er—your call?"

"On Terry?" Les grinned self-consciously. "He'll be glad o' seein' me, Reverend. Practically left the old garage to me, 'specially market days."

Shaw tasted his tea which Les had poured, and almost gagged on the sweetness. He must have shovelled the sugar in. He dithered at the new problem, desperately wondering how to wangle a cup without sugar. He'd heard that prisoners and people in detention went frantic for sweet foods and drink.

"Er, will you leave it till Monday?" he begged, fumbling to invent a reason. "Um, the Lord's Day . . ."

"Oh." Les nodded soberly. "'Course, Reverend. Sorry. I forgot, like."

"Thank you, Les."

"Plenty to do at home anyway," Les said confidently.

"Er, shouldn't I phone Sergeant Sheldon first?"

"Why, Reverend?"

The priest stared across the table in disbelief. Taunton honestly was ignorant of any difficulties. It was as if the terrible events of the dark hours, macabre as they had been, had never occurred at all.

"Last night, Les. You remember?"

Les laughed sheepishly and sawed his egg. "Yes, Reverend. A right old game, warn't it?"

"Do you feel you—er—can go home?"

"O' course. Only across the playing field."

Shaw leaned away, exasperated. "But is it safe, Les?"

"Safe? You mean the lads?"

"Certainly. By all accounts they were after your skin."

Les laughed, nodding vigorously. His appetite was unimpaired, though his scratches and lesions showed horribly. "They'd had a few, Reverend. They get like that."

"Hadn't you best wait, see how folk react?"

"Mean no harm. I seen 'em duck some lads in the pond." He guffawed. "I helped. I were one of 'em."

"Look, Les. I'm only concerned."

"Don't you bother your head, Reverend."

And Taunton wolfed his breakfast, clearing a mound of bread and drinking pints of tea grotesquely sweetened while the priest observed and worried. The man seemed curiously unaffected by it all. The malice, the extent of the village's animosity towards himself, simply went unrecognized. The man was like a simpleton—could he be? Or so incredibly innocent by nature that even the most transparent guile was beyond him? The priest rose to clear the table, for once wishing he had the wisdom to instil a little mistrust into this man.

CHAPTER 12

George Falconer decided against taking Night Owl and the cart up to the White Hart, a fact he was to regret even though the itinerant pickers' children who haunted the pubs would have made her life a misery while waiting. Night Owl was a great excuse for leaving on time—or even early.

To his astonishment the lay preacher and his wife were seated on one of the tavern benches outside on the forecourt. Naturally, neither had a drink.

"Good day, Nathaniel, Zuleika."

"Good day, Councillor." Neither smiled. The honorific slowed George's steps.

"You want me, Nathaniel?"

"I do."

"As does the rest of the village, Councillor," Zuleika added gravely. "We are bearers of a petition for goodness against foul living."

"Well," George sighed, "I'll bring out a jar. We might as well settle it out here. I take it you'll not sit indoors?"

"The Lord's air is sweeter than in that house of drunkards, Councillor," Zuleika said. George nodded at the reproach, but found his father's reply on his tongue unbidden.

"Ar, Zuleika. But as we are more than two and presumably gathered in His Name . . . I'll not be a minute."

He ignored their scandalized gasp and pushed into the public bar, noting Eric Carnforth and Joe Sheldon against the bar. They looked round resignedly as he ordered a pint of bitter from Dorothy Benham.

"You'll need this, George," Dorothy informed him. "Mr. and Mrs. Jones have been waiting this past hour."

"And I thought the weather'd improved, Dorothy," he said, gloomily asking the two men, "Coming out?"

"Unfortunately."

They trooped over to where the composed pair sat. Joe dragged another bench over and Eric pulled a table for them to lean on.

"Anyone else to come?" George asked Eric.

"No. Sarah Horn's trying to persuade Fogg Powell and the Henriques to sign the petition. They might."

Two of the three biggest farmers in the village would indeed be a catch.

"And Mrs. Davidson?" George asked mischievously, winking at the policeman.

"Nobody mentioned calling at Hall Farm," Eric replied, straightfaced. Mrs. Davidson's affair with Bertie, her principal farm labourer and now her foreman, was a perennial source of scandal to the village. Nothing was less likely than Mrs. Horn visiting Hall Farm.

"It's the petition. Something must be done." Nathaniel rapped the table, his preacher's trick.

Ed Edgeworth slipped on to the bench beside Zuleika. He

had a full pint and must have followed them out of the public bar.

"How do, Ed." George was relieved to welcome the school-teacher. He would have been more useful had he spoken up at the meeting last night, though, he thought carpingly. Maybe then matters wouldn't have got this far. What's needed is cool common sense and this young teacher seemed to have plenty.

"I'm not aware your opinion's welcome or asked for," Nathaniel Jones said sonorously.

Ed grimaced disarmingly and picked up George's tobacco pouch to fill his own pipe. "You'll hear it anyway, Reverend."

"I'm a lay preacher!" Nathaniel's mouth tightened in rage. "Not an instrument of an establishment parasitic upon religion!"

"Preaching's your big chance, though." Ed blew his smoke away from the others and returned George his pouch. "Ta, George. There'll be you in your pulpit—"

"Pulpit? I don't set myself higher than my fellow man!"

"—And Reverend Watson in his," Ed continued. "You against Taunton coming home, Watson for it. A right tug o'war."

"Cool it, Ed," Joe Sheldon ordered. "This is serious."

Ed's levity vanished. His eyes glinted. "What makes you think I'm not serious, Joe?"

"All right, all right. But this petition."

Nathaniel spoke incisively, addressing George and Eric exclusively. "The wish of the village is that Taunton be prevented from coming back here. Unanimous."

"I didn't sign it," Ed intruded. "Nor, I hear, did Dr. Salford. And Reverend Watson gave him shelter."

"Pra-cti-call-ee a consensus," Nathaniel intoned.

"To the council," Zuleika added. "Hand it over, Nathaniel."

The preacher placed a sheaf of assorted papers on the trestle table. "Officially handed over."

"Thank you." George sighed as he passed it to Eric Carn-forth. "Look after it, Eric."

"Look after . . . ?" Nathaniel shook his head decisively.

"That will not do. It isn't to be slept on, Councillor. Action's needed. We want the village council to *act*."

"To do what?"

"That's for the council to decide."

"I asked exactly *how* the council can act," Ed cut in, sharply now. "This man's been declared innocent. Any action against him's against the law."

The preacher faced him. "He was not innocent."

"He was released."

"There is a difference."

Ed turned angrily to the police sergeant. "*Is* there a difference, Joe?"

"In the *results* of the law, what it means to the status of the individual, no difference at all."

"So the village can do sod all," Ed concluded. He raised his bitter to the preacher and his wife. "Cheers."

"Less of that, Ed." George was unhappy at having to admonish so popular a figure as the young teacher, especially as every word of this conversation would be relayed throughout the village by nightfall. "Joe. Has this petition any force at all?"

"On the village council, it can force you to discuss the matter."

"But on Taunton?"

"No." Joe was as unhappy as George. "He has the same protection in law as you, as the schoolchildren, as—well—as anybody else."

"Scandalous!" Zuleika exclaimed, rising. "Come on, Nathaniel."

"That can't be."

Observing Nathaniel's calm certainty, Ed felt uneasy as he stood to let Zuleika pass.

"It is, Nathaniel," Joe repeated. "Seek further legal advice if you wish—"

"Come, Nathaniel." Zuleika gazed calmly at the seated men. "This clique is against all sanity. We'll appeal elsewhere."

"What for?" Ed asked, glancing at the policeman, but Joe avoided his eye.

"For?" The preacher waited a theatrical moment before replying. "For guidance *and* support."

The couple stalked across the forecourt and off down the Colnebridge road, making a passing car hoot in alarm.

"Time we had the footpaths laid, George," Eric Carnforth said forlornly, following their determined progress.

"Cost," George answered mechanically.

Ed lost patience. "About Taunton," he reminded them. "You said nothing, Eric."

Eric shrugged and took a draught from his pint. "I'm only the clerk. I've no real authority."

"You've a tongue in your head."

"It's easy for you, Ed. You're an incomer. You can go."

"Funny. I'd not thought of that," the schoolteacher said with wonderment. And it was true. He hadn't. He asked, "Where are you from, George?"

"Here. Village born and bred."

"Eric?"

"Beckholt. Same class as George at school."

"Nathaniel and Zuleika? Sarah Horn?"

"Here, too. Miseries years ago, too."

Ed pursed his lips. "Joe's a Colnebridge man, right?" At Joe's puzzled nod he continued, "Then we'll make Joe our referee. Let's call the Beckholt locals protagonists. Now." He leant forwards. "Who are the opposites, the antagonists?"

"What's he on about?" Eric asked of the others.

Ed drove on. "Me. From Birmingham. The doctor—she's from Kendal. Reverend Watson . . . anybody know?"

"Shropshire."

"It's a pattern! Can't you see?" Ed's excitement caused a passing couple to turn, smiling. "It's the age-old contest between local prerogative and the acceptance of legislative powers centralized for the greater good of society!"

"Cock," Eric said bluntly, and rose. "I'm off. Let me know what to do with this, George." He swept up the petition papers.

"Nothing Eric," Ed answered for George. "Please."

"I hope you don't teach our children that crap, Ed."

"I do, Eric. I do."

Ed reached again for George Falconer's pouch for a last fill but the smallholder deftly removed and pocketed it. He grinned at Ed, trying to make a joke out of the refusal.

"Get your own," he said. "*Incomer!*" He too rose and accompanied Eric off the pub forecourt.

"You'll get yourself in trouble, young lad," the policeman said, watching them go.

"Somebody has to say it, Joe. And I'm right."

Joe downed the rest of his drink. "Maybe, Ed."

"Only *maybe*? And that from you, our guardian?" Ed shook his head in mock despair. "I was going to offer you another pint till you said that."

"Him being out changes things, Ed."

"How?"

Joe grinned, openly, for the first time. "You keep asking how, how this, how that. Out here in a village like Beckholt, there is no *how*. Face it."

"Balls, Joe. Look around." Ed indicated that the half-dozen parked cars, the passing bus from Dragonswell heading crowded into town, the open fields and orchards to the north and the village houses to the south. "Listen. A juke-box. The latest records. Over there the football team knocking posts in for this afternoon. Over here a score of visitors boozing their way to a cheap ploughman's dinner. It's . . . it's *ordinary*, Joe. Your actual average rural society."

"Balls, Ed," Joe gave back and calmly gazed about. "And now *you* look around. None of those cars belongs here. They're the cars of strangers, throughcomers. That Dragonswell bus is crowded—right. Oh, it'll pick up our own village people. But they'll sit on one side at the front. They'll not mix with the Dragonswell folk, not at any price." He grinned at the teacher's expression. "Didn't you realize that? No? Of course not. But then, how often have you travelled on it, Ed? Don't bother—I know the answer: twice. Once when your motor went in for servicing, and on Easter Sunday this year. Trouble with a spare tyre, wasn't it?"

"That proves—"

"And folk in the White Hart, playing the juke-box. All
strangers. Peapickers. Holidaymakers and gipsies. And why? Because Dorothy and Jim are busy paying off their stock default
from last summer. They'll take any customers for a year or two.
Then they'll exclude the visitors like Malcolm and Margaret at
the Treble Tile, and Del and Jenny Tree at the Queen's Head."

"I don't see what this proves, Joe."

"And the football team," Joe continued relentlessly, pointing
towards the field opposite. Enthusiastic shouts were crossing the
intervening distance.

"Everybody in these islands has played football for thousands
of years," Ed insisted. "So?"

"So the preparations for today's game look innocent enough."
Joe smiled. The schoolteacher detected with something of a
shock the sorrow in the police sergeant's voice. "But the game
will be a bloodbath. It's our village against Fieldham, the next
village."

"A typical local derby."

"No, Ed. Our lads'll try to kick the others silly. And vice
versa. Tonight there'll be a holocaust. Here. All three pubs. You
know what they shout, our footballers, when they split a Fieldham lad's head open? 'Fax 'im—no, not *fix* him. 'Fax. Fairfax."

"Who?"

"Head of the Parliamentarians at the Colnebridge siege,
1648. Cromwell's boss in the Great Civil War. Beckholt was for
Parliament, Fieldham helped Royalists. Your 'actual average
rural society' is composed entirely of incomers, Ed."

"You make it sound so . . . primitive."

Joe nodded, more sad than portentous. "It is primitive, Ed.
And now . . ."

"Yes?" Ed asked guardedly.

Joe grinned. "I'll have a pint, please. Thanks for asking."

"Typical bloody copper!"

CHAPTER 13

"Mick Robie!"

Joe Sheldon slowed his car to walking pace beside the big man.

"Hello, Joe. Busy?"

"Hang on." The policeman braked and got out, somewhat against his better judgement. It was unusual for Mick to be walking alone, even the few hundred yards between the social club and the Queen's Head. He remarked this, and Robie grinned.

"The lads just aren't about today," he said, unabashed.

"Maybe they don't want your company, Mick."

"Impossible!" Robie framed his face with huge hands, laughing. "I'm always wanted, Joe. You can see why!"

"Never seen you on your tod before, though."

Robie dropped his flippancy. "Heard the lads had a hard night."

"Did you have a hard night, too, Mick Robie?"

"Not me. Not in that sense o' the word, Joe."

"Can you prove it?"

Robie became truculent. "Don't have to, Sherlock. But if you insisted . . ."

"I caught Frank and Bob doing over Les Taunton's cottage. They'll be up before the magistrate. There were others who ran off. Too dark."

"Dear me, Joe. What is this village coming to?"

"Where were you?"

"Queen's Head. Till closing time."

"I'll check that with Del Tree," the policeman warned.

"No, don't," Robie replied evenly. "Check with Jenny. She'll remember best."

Joe got back into the panda car, defeated. The meeting at the White Hart and checking Mick Robie would make him late for dinner now, the one thing that made Eileen mad as hell. Further down the road he waved as he caught sight of old Stan Deller out walking, slowly nowadays and, the policeman in him noted, affecting a heavy ash walking-stick. Nothing in that, probably. People said his condition was going along fine. Old Stan waved in return, doing it with his stick. Therefore he couldn't need it all that much. At least, not for walking.

So Jenny would alibi Mick Robie. Don't ask Del, ask his missus.

Stan Deller turned in at Mrs. Winner's gate, its latch defective as always. Now, if only he was up to it he could have fixed it, easy as anything. Maybe done himself a bit of good with Hilda Winner. Still shapely, a mature East Anglian figure with breasts that would squeeze out between a man's fingers just the way God intended. Been alone these five years, since Winner went down on that coastal barge in the winter gales.

He tapped up the path, deliberately noisy with his stick. Always gentlemanly to let a woman know you are coming. He chuckled inwardly at the double meaning, and went round to the back door. The mark of a friendly neighbour. Mrs. Winner was baking, he saw with some annoyance.

"Come in, Mr. Deller. Sit you down. I'm behind with myself today."

"You bake on Tuesdays," he accused.

"I wanted a change." She wiped her floury hands on her apron. "I'll make you coffee."

"I could do with some nice bread."

"Not likely. I'd have that pretty doctor after me, and Nurse Batsford. You and your diabetes."

"A taste," he wheedled.

"You'll get coffee with no sugar and powdered milk, and like it."

He sat heavily on the stool by the kitchen door to look out at the garden. "There was trouble last night."

"All noise and no sense." Mrs. Winner was obviously prepared to dismiss the events, but for some reason he wanted to pursue them.

"Were you all right? I saw him come round."

"Of course I was."

He glanced at her slyly. "What was all that shouting then?"

"If you really want to know, Stanley Deller, it was a stupid woman who'd talked herself into a screaming fit." She slammed the kettle on and spooned instant coffee into two mugs. "That's what comes of listening to people."

"Then what was he snooping—?"

She faced him, practically blaming him. "He'd come for his cat, Mr. Deller."

"So he said."

"If I'd half the sense I was born with, I'd have just popped her out to him."

"You did right, locking the door. His sort can't be trusted."

"*Trusting* is different, Mr. Deller. Being sensible's a body's obligation, to herself and everybody else. I needn't have let him in."

"The lads gave him what for. He's hid at the priest's."

"Senseless. Just senseless."

"You didn't say that when poor Olive Hanwell got killed, Mrs. Winner."

"The law had it all in hand," Hilda reprimanded. "That too was different from running about in the darkness acting like lunatics, breaking cottages down."

"Folk say he'll come back in any case."

Hilda Winner felt a twinge of apprehension despite her fine words. "When?"

"Today. Maybe tomorrow." He was gauging her reaction carefully. She crossed to unplug the kettle.

"Well," she said, thrown on the defensive by her instinctive fear. "Sergeant Sheldon will keep an eye on him."

"Didn't help poor Olive any."

"It's changed since then." She poured the hot water and stirred vigorously. "Les Taunton's been cleared."

"Then let the judge have him as *his* next-door neighbour."

Hilda sat with the old man. She had a few minutes to spare, having not folded her flour in yet. The garden was in a fair way. Good potato yield this year, though trampled as Les Taunton had rushed through them in the night to escape from the hooligans. Poor Les.

Yes, poor Les. She was approaching middle age, if forty was middle age. Odd how a woman's feelings led her on and how she couldn't quite judge what she was doing, or even what she was intending, until it was too late. Or only *seemed* too late? That was the utter foolishness every woman had in her make-up, the burdensome inability to assess her own designs.

Looking back on the time Les Taunton came here first, setting about the old thatched cottage next door as if his life depended on it and slaving all hours to knock it into shape, her reactions were probably typical. A lonely woman without her own man any longer. A pleasant-looking lad, ten—all right—happen fifteen—years younger. Strong and whistling. What more natural than that she should pass him a few things she made? Working part-time up at Mrs. Davidson's at Hall Farm had taught her that high and low, rich and poor, shared a commonality of the human condition. Mrs. Davidson was a nice enough woman, though spoiled somewhat, who enjoyed—yes obviously and unashamedly enjoyed—her first cowhand's ministrations in a scandalous way. Though was it not only a more honest way?

Because, Hilda Winner, there had been a time you came perilously close to running your hands through Les Taunton's thick hair, and might have gone farther than that. The poor man's practically a simpleton, so unused to women that innuendo went over his head unnoticed. A woman would have to undress herself, and him most probably, and instruct the silly slow buffoon in the ways of men and women before he'd even understand.

"Mrs. Winner?" Old Mr. Deller was talking.

"I'm sorry. I didn't quite catch that."

"I said I'll mend your latch. The gate."

"Don't be silly, Mr. Deller. I'll get round to it."

"You'll need to be extra careful."

"The stupid gate's only knee high."

She rose to her kitchen table. When Les Taunton had been taken by Sergeant Sheldon to "help police with enquiries," she had dismissed the whole thing as ridiculous. For some days after the first thrilling astonishment, she told people that Les Taunton couldn't do a thing like that, it was impossible, Les Taunton wouldn't hurt a fly. Then as the newspapers took up the story suspicions hardened into possibilities and theories became certainty. Maybe a woman should think always of her own instinctive reactions to a man, keep a hold on what she had seen and learned of him. But a whole village knew best . . . didn't it? Yet it hadn't behaved sensibly last night. Like something out of the Wild West or the dark days of past ages when folk were half-mad with superstition. It was never sheer force which changed you. Only those words which nudged suggestively in your mind until you, too, found yourself reasoning in a way you'd have thought impossible before.

Les Taunton was chased from his own home in the night while she had huddled indoors, listening in horror to the smashes and the final mad scrabbling in her garden as somebody had blundered, sobbing for breath, across her favourite flowers. She wondered how he was managing at the priest's house, that great barn of a rectory that was too poor to hire a daily woman to see to the place.

Clare had carefully planned when best to send Esther Batsford to see to Taunton.

"Nurse Batsford. Could you see to this, please?"

"Yes, Doctor."

"It's only one visit. The rectory."

"Reverend Watson?"

"No. His visitor."

Clare prevented herself quickly looking up at the changed tone. She passed the slip over and thankfully sipped her coffee to give the district nurse time to read Taunton's name and adjust to the idea. The nurse always called at the surgery to complete her records of house visits and report any major problems over coffee. What with doctors and nurses and "killer" refugees abounding, she thought in irritation, the Reverend Shaw Watson, that renowned spiritual pillar of Beckholt, would never again have such an opportunity for spiritual glory, straight from the storybook of Christian ethics.

No hesitation but a slight changed tone. "Taunton?"

"I'm afraid so. You heard of the bother, I take it."

"People keep asking me about him."

"It's as well you know nothing, then." She narrated the events of the night. "He needs his injuries dressed. The record's in the file."

"Can I look?"

"Please do." She poured another cup while the district nurse scanned the envelope's contents, and asked, "Did you know Taunton before this trouble, Nurse?"

"Not really. I vaguely remember a sprain or something. Yes. It's here."

"Anything else?"

"Nothing. It'd be here if there was, wouldn't it?"

"Probably. One thing . . . why do you suppose he ran to the priest's house?"

"I don't know." Nurse Batsford bent over the envelope again though she had read it quickly through once and it was bare enough. "Isn't it natural, Doctor?"

Clare watched the girl's head, still poring over the cards. "Why 'natural'?"

"Well. A priest, the church. I don't know."

"You mean sanctuary?" This assumption was beginning to irritate.

"Perhaps that. Maybe it was just the nearest place."

"But that's the point, Nurse. *This* is the nearest place. The surgery. We are as little likely to surrender him to a crowd of hooligans as any priest, surely?"

"Maybe he came here and you were . . ." The nurse flushed and tried uncomfortably to rescue the sentence from such a gaffe. ". . . Sometimes a doctor's off duty. Most villagers know now about the cover arrangements with Dr. Greig."

"I *was* out. But Taunton ran straight to the priest's." Clare pressed on, "Not to the church. Not to Sergeant Sheldon's. Straight to the rectory."

"I suppose it was just chance, Doctor. Or . . ."

"Or deliberate," Clare concluded, cruelly for her. "Like every other action in existence, either chance or deliberate."

Nurse Batsford, examining the uninformative record, still did not look up to meet the doctor's eyes but was stung into a retort. "I was going to say maybe Les Taunton *chose* to run there."

"To the rectory?"

"No. To—the priest."

"To Reverend Shaw Watson. To him." Clare found the possibility infuriating, and as swift concealment took the envelope and its cards from the nurse and shuffled them into order. "Yet he didn't know the priest."

"He wasn't a regular attender, I believe." The nurse was very sure of this, Clare noted mentally.

So the doctor had checked up on it with somebody else, Esther Batsford registered. The observation misled her into speaking unguardedly. "Shaw says hardly anybody is these days."

"Does he really?" Clare said casually. "First names."

"I've heard he says that." Nurse Batsford's colour heightened. She scribbled a reminder on her notepad. "I'd better get on."

"Taunton's had his tetanus booster."

"Thank you. I saw it entered. Is there anything else, Doctor?"

"No, thank you. Oh. Mr. Deller. I called on him for a look at his ocular fundi. He's no change on last time. But is he any more reliable with his insulin and his diet than he was?"

The district nurse smiled, on safer ground. "He's much better now than he was. Dr. Chesterton used to say, 'You can trust Deller implicitly, Nurse, as far as you can throw him.' Mr. Deller's average."

"Thank you, Nurse. I hope the rest of the day's quiet."

"Do you want me to call back, Doctor?"

"No need, Nurse."

Clare gave her a bright smile and watched her go. We're full of other people's sayings today, she thought uncharitably as the door closed. On impulse she picked up the receiver and dialled Ken's duty number.

"This is Dr. Salford, Inspector. Am I free to speak in confidence?"

"Yes, Clare. All clear this end. No trouble?"

"Nothing like that," she said impatiently. "Ken. Last night's business. This Taunton. He ran from a crowd of hooligans who attacked his cottage—"

"Sheldon took two of the yobbos in charge."

"Yes, yes. He ran to the priest's house."

"I have the report. What's the question?"

"Not to the policeman's house, not to the surgery, Ken. That's the question. Why?"

"Why not?"

"Because he doesn't know him, that's why not. And he does know Sergeant Sheldon. And other places are nearer."

"Does it matter? Probably some primitive instinct—"

"In the Middle Ages, maybe. But these days, Ken? When religion's on the way out? And the bloody priest's useless?"

"Taunton was probably too scared to think."

"Ken. One thing. About the evidence, at Taunton's trial."

"All circumstantial, really. He'd been seen talking with her, walking near the pond. Plenty of witnesses for that. Then he was seen going home."

"By Mr. Deller?"

"That's right."

"With the girl?"

"No, but it was alleged she was going to meet him. She was seen going into his garden at dusk—"

"Again by Deller?"

"Yes. Nothing wrong with that. At the social club she'd told people she was seeing Les. Probably arranged to visit his cottage instead, on the sly." His chuckle came against her ear. "Girls have been known to do that sort of thing."

"Stop laughing," she told him sharply. "I'm serious. And did she come out?"

"No. Deller testified he'd watched continuously but she never emerged. And the lights never came on in Taunton's place."

"All night?"

"Certainly all evening at least. Deller turned in at midnight. He could recollect the last programme in enough detail to be convincing."

"So if Olive spent the evening and possibly all night in a darkened cottage with the—with Taunton, how did he manage to get off?"

"Deller *could* have dozed. And Olive died about elevenish."

"That same night?"

"Correct. Found at eleven-thirty by a chap's dog."

"Which chap?"

"No use, Clare. Two men, neighbours, walking their dogs at night. Corroborative alibis for the whole night, visitors at their respective homes and all."

"And what did Taunton do all evening?"

"Says he walked with Olive at dusk—that's the fully witnessed bit. Then says he went home and waited for her, read and listened to the radio—"

"—In the dark?"

"So he said. Olive didn't show up, so he went to bed. Sheldon woke him next morning. Sergeant Hawksmoor from Central handled it. And quite well, too. Must have looked cut and dried."

"Thanks, Ken."

"Clare? Why the interest?"

She didn't know and said so. Her sense of acute dissatisfaction was as disturbing as ever. She did not want to continue talking.

"See you Tuesday night?" he questioned.

"Probably."

"Only probably? Have you changed your on-call duty?"

"Not so far." She knew she would be looking for an argument with him if she continued the conversation. "I have to go, Ken. See you soon."

"See you, Clare."

She sat for a while staring at the phone. Something was badly wrong. Wrong with Ken's summary, wrong with the evidence, wrong with the village's reaction, with Taunton's account, wrong with everything.

The image came of Esther Batsford caring for Taunton and chatting happily in the rectory with that indecisive bumbling fool of a priest. And was something wrong with *that* cosy little scene, too, despite all those first names? Clare pushed the unfiled medical envelopes into an untidy heap, knowing that finding them disorderly would only irritate herself more later on and send Jackie Hughes into one of her famous sulks.

She found her car keys and handbag and looked up Dr. Chesterton's number in Frinton-on-Sea.

CHAPTER 14

The brewer's dray was unloading at the White Hart. The two shire horses had already been given their pints of bitter and Dorothy Benham was standing talking on the forecourt with the drayman when Dr. Salford's car passed.

"Odd time o'day," she said.

"For what?"

"The doctor to be out. Must be an emergency or something."

"Marvellous job." The drayman spat expertly, missing the off leader's hoof by an inch.

"Bad as a publican's, on at all hours."

"You don't know you're born, love." The drayman took his tip from her and pouched it, grinning. "I get more down the Queen's Head."

"Everybody gets more down the Queen's Head," Dorothy said wisely.

"Bonny girl like you—"

"Ugly bloke like you." She smiled as she topped him and flounced indoors.

Andy Greig had been displeased. Clare drove towards the coast working out her repayments to Andy for covering for the rest of the day until evening surgery. He'd asked what for.

"What's the matter? That priest who phoned?"

"Certainly *not* him!"

"Keep your hair on, Clare. I'll stand by. Will you tell the telephone exchange?"

She promised to do so and got the car out. By then she had contacted Dr. Chesterton and successfully inveigled him into inviting her to stop by for tea. For once he wasn't out on the golf-course. He said how glad he'd be to see her, but that was only average for an elderly retired man, practically at his last gasp, who spent most days knocking little white balls into holes.

She drove on, wondering about men and what strange creatures they were. For some reason she found herself going the wrong way, having automatically turned northwards towards Dragonswell. She tut-tutted in annoyance. She could afford the extra minute or two, but didn't particularly want to pass the rectory again.

The car slowed, seemingly of its own accord, at the rectory gate. Esther Batsford's bicycle was leaning on the gate-post and her dressing case was gone, so presumably the district nurse was already inside and doing her stuff. She'd pedalled round with some alacrity, Clare remembered mildly. Perhaps making certain that one particular worm didn't escape too far?

As she accelerated towards the White Hart crossroads she caught sight of a woman's figure walking briskly towards the rectory, using the far gate which met the public footpath towards the playing fields. Mrs. Winner, Les Taunton's neighbour. Now, why? Wasn't she the one whose screams reputedly provoked the yobbos to further excesses last night?

By the White Hart Clare saw Dorothy Benham signing the drayman's delivery sheet, and thought, let her wonder where I'm going. It was high time she did pay a visit to Dr. Chesterton. It might clear the air. Passing George Falconer's roadside stall, she saw Ed Edgeworth chatting to the elderly councillor and helping him to restock his stall with celery and carrots while doing so. She wound the window down and gave both a casual and impartial wave. The schoolteacher looked after her car, she saw in the driving mirror with some satisfaction. Why couldn't the priest be brisk and assertive as Ed? And as popular?

She was sick of the village and its entanglements, and all the way to Colnebridge bypass she left the window open to feel the breeze lift her hair.

"How is he?" the priest asked.

"Fine," Esther Batsford answered. "No oil painting, but he'll live." She was doing the washing-up, a contribution which both exasperated and worried Shaw.

He asked doubtfully, "Should you be doing that?"

"Afraid I'll ask more than the going rate?"

"No. Of course not. Only—" He realized she was smiling. A joke. She'd meant it as a joke. He grinned, reddening. "Only you came to see to Les Taunton."

"He's soaking those dressings off. It'll take a minute."

"Well, thanks." He took a tea towel and started on the plates.

"Leave them," the nurse advised. "They drain clean anyway with these washing up liquids. Saves no end of time. Just do the cutlery. They go streaky."

"Is that true?" he asked, surprised.

She laughed, busy at the sink. "You're funny, Shaw. It's obvious. And it saves your tea-cloths."

"I'll remember in future."

She paused, sudsy hands on the bowl's rim. "Why don't you have somebody in?"

He was instantly on the defensive. "It's money, I'm afraid. So many things come down to money these days."

"They needn't." She resumed briskly. "There are volunteers."

"It's . . . well, charity, that, isn't it?"

"Charity's quite honourable."

"Y-e-s," he agreed slowly. "But how would it work?"

"You'd have a rota. Each could do a little bit of the housework, perhaps cook now and then."

"Would that not be, well, open to misinterpretation?"

"Not if there were several, arranging it among themselves."

"And they're so busy."

"Rubbish." She dried her hands, looking around to see all was done. "They're on their bottoms most of the day. They *say* they're hard done by, but that's the party line of the idle housewife. My grannie used to say, A woman's work is never done when it never gets started! And it'd do them good."

"Would it really?" He was still doubtful.

"As long as you don't have just one." She finished the cutlery for him and hung up the tea towel. "Especially Jane Lang's sort."

"She's been ill, anyway."

"And don't we all know it," Esther said drily. "I'm her district nurse, remember? That woman makes an industry of an ailment. Thank goodness Dr. Salford stands no nonsense from her sort. Dr. Greig's the softest touch in the Eastern Hundreds."

"That was kind of you, er . . . er . . ."

"Esther," the nurse prompted pleasantly. "Try it."

"Yes—er, Esther."

In the living-room where Les Taunton was obediently sitting, his hands wrapped in moist cloths, the radio was playing loudly. They paused in the hallway by silent mutual consent. Esther spoke quietly.

"You didn't mind harbouring Taunton last night, Shaw?"

"Why, no. He wasn't very comfortable. The settee—"

"You weren't scared?"

"Not really." He shrugged. "Not much choice."

"About Dr. Salford. Did you and she have words?"

"A row? No. Nothing like that. Only . . ."

"Yes?"

"She wasn't too pleased." He shrugged unhappily. "Maybe it was my calling her out when she was off duty." He scuffed the worn carpet with a shoe. "Perhaps I shouldn't have gone round there."

"I see." The nurse gauged his embarrassment and spoke candidly. "She hasn't a lot of time for most other people, Shaw. Oh, she's a good doctor. Fine. But everything to her is factual, clear cut—or it's not worth bothering about."

"People like me?"

"Like *all* priests, *all* religions, Shaw."

"I know I'm no ball of fire, Esther." He tried to smile, indicating with a jerk of his head the living-room from which loud wordless singing was audible as Taunton tried to join in an unfamiliar melody. "In fact, I've more doubts than most. When somebody crammed full of technology like Dr. Salford faces me I feel so . . . so inadequate. A fraud, even." His eyes met hers. "So much of my place here in the village is trust, simple trusting in anything which folk guess I might represent. You see, I have no technology. The church has no instruments, no drugs, nothing. We might . . . *I* might be one colossal myth."

"Or not." Esther was no longer smiling.

"Or not. But I can't be sure."

"Then try to *look* sure," the girl urged with some exasperation. "Taunton came running to *you* for protection, nowhere else."

"It isn't lack of belief," Shaw explained as if to himself. "It's that I can't be businesslike with others."

"Then pretend. Let your convictions show."

He grinned, embarrassed. "You're one to talk. You're a technocrat."

"Maybe it's medical technology which is the great modern myth. Ever thought of that?"

"Yes," he answered frankly. "But without conviction."

"Shaw, you're hopeless?"

He reached out as if to take her arm but smiled ruefully and let it fall. "You're one to talk, Nurse," he chided. They moved towards the living-room. "Giving a priest religious instruction."

The doorbell rang as Esther spread sterile towels on the side table prior to peeling off Les Taunton's dressings. Shaw opened the door to Hilda Winner.

"Good day to you, Reverend."

"Er, good day, Mrs. Winner. Do, erm, won't you come in?"

She remained on the step. "I came to call on Les Taunton, if you please, Reverend."

"He's inside with Nurse Batsford. Go on through."

The woman drew breath and entered, throwing a practised glance around the hall and vestibule as she did so.

"Good day, Nurse."

Esther was as surprised as Taunton. "Hello, Mrs. Winner. I'll not be long—"

"No need, Nurse. It'll only take a moment." Hilda stood before the settee looking down at the apprehensive man.

"Hello, Mrs. Winner," he offered cautiously.

"Hello, Les." The woman had obviously steeled herself for the encounter and delivered the words in a rushed monotone. "I came to tell you I was sorry about last night's misunderstanding. You came for your cat. I realize that. She's well and you can have her when you go back to your cottage, if you choose to. Are you hurt any?"

"No, Mrs. Winner."

"He'll mend," Esther put in.

"Right, then." The woman gave an abrupt nod at the priest. "Is there anything I can do, Nurse?"

"Nothing, thank you."

The woman looked from Esther to the patient and back. She hesitated, adding carefully to Les, "I'll not need to call again here, then. If you want anything buying in, you can let me know."

"There, Les!" Esther said brightly, using the remark to lift a soaked dressing. "That's an offer you can't refuse! Isn't that kind, Shaw?" She darted a quick smile at the visitor.

"Indeed."

"Thanks, Mrs. Winner."

Hilda seemed more at ease, even pleased by the words said. "It's no hardship."

Shaw saw her to the door.

"I'm pleased you came, Mrs. Winner." He obviously meant it.

"No more than I, Reverend," she said, obviously meaning that in return.

She walked off briskly down the gravelled drive.

A crate of brown ale had been brought into the football pavilion. The team was busy wasting their chances early by passing flagon bottles around. Frank and Bob were morose and heavy-headed in a corner, having changed into strip early and managed to grab a bottle between them.

"What d'you reckon we'll get?"

"Oh, a fine, bound over," Frank guessed.

"I'll get done," Bob said gloomily. "That magistrate bound me over last time I went up. The bastard'll go berserk."

"That car?"

"Only a bit of a laugh, me and Harry."

Harry, Bob's cousin and the team's flying winger, heard his name mentioned and pushed through the mob of changing footballers.

"Bad lads," he ribbed. "You'll catch it."

"Too right we will," Bob said. "Especially me."

"I heard Mick scarpered." Harry was grinning as he lifted their flagon for a swig. "Good old Mick."

"We were round the back," Frank grumbled. "Catched."

"Couldn't see Joe Sheldon coming, the bastard."

"You silly sods." Harry skillfully kept the bottle out of his cousin's reach.

"We meant no harm."

"Don't tell me, Bob. Tell the beak."

The pair groaned.

"Not Mick's fault," Frank groused. "We were all in it."

"There's one whose fault it is." Bob got the bottle at last and drank.

"That bloody killer," Harry agreed.

"Don't know why nobody's taken him out before now."

"If Olive Hanwell had any family worth speaking of—"

"It's the bastard law," Bob muttered. "So bloody namby-pamby it pesters the life out of us but lets a bloody killer go free."

"*And* has us up, just for worrittin' him."

A murmur of agreement made them realize others of the team had been listening. The trainer interrupted to urge the team out onto the pitch. He had enough worries over today's important decider without wanting to listen to local rubbishy gossip. He'd watched the Fieldham team arrive. Only twenty-odd supporters, but their forwards looked fitter than he had ever seen them in previous years.

"And who fetched that bloody beer?" he yelled angrily.

"Not me, Josh."

"Well, it was bloody somebody!" he bawled, seizing bottles and slamming them down on the benches. "Get moving, you idle sods. And if you dare lose . . ."

The team ran out in a mood of surly bitterness.

CHAPTER 15

Dr. Chesterton's house stood well back from the seafront road at Frinton. The diminutive church on the corner was thronged with visitors as Clare drove past and swung to a stop outside the walled garden. Chesterton was working in the garden, cutting at the shrubs with large secateurs.

"Welcome to Geriatrics Anonymous!" he called. "Helen! See who's here!"

"Hello, John." Clare gave him a peck. "I feel on holiday."

"Take my tip, young Salford," he lectured with mock seriousness. "When you get that feeling, hang on to it. Don't go back! Stay here."

"Pleased with life, John?"

"Delighted! Retiring was the best day's work I ever did."

"Hello, Clare! Marvellous to see you." Helen Chesterton

came down the steps to greet her effusively. "Yes, we're thoroughly adjusted to indolence. We don't jump when the phone rings."

"How lovely!"

"And any visitor's a major event."

"Hush, John!" Helen scolded. "Clare will think we're old fogies. But I *have* made some scones in your honour. They *may* be all right. Fingers crossed, everyone!" She hurried ahead, calling that she would bring tea out to the conservatory alcove. "Get your medical gossip over with, both of you!" she ordered over her shoulder. "I'll expect only humane conversation over tea, or you'll not deserve any scones at all. Do you hear?"

"Fat-free," Chesterton whispered furtively to Clare. "All part of her plan to keep atherosclerosis at bay."

Clare was smiling, instantly at rest under the influence of the old doctor's good-humoured inanities.

"I should have come to see you a lot earlier," she said, realizing the truth of her words the moment she spoke. "You make me feel better already."

"Why do you say that?" Chesterton said disingenuously. "Were you feeling worse?"

"Oh, not really." Clare flopped into a canvas chair.

"I can have the phone disconnected for an hour, if you like."

She laughed at his joke. "Your famous deputizing system is in operation."

"Thank goodness! I had visions of the Black Death rampaging without medical assistance."

"Nothing so innocuous."

"Good heavens, Clare!" He sat opposite where he could face the sea. "Whatever's going on in that village? The moment I turn my back you let it go to rack and ruin. Ah," he sighed theatrically, "you young, unlearned doctors. Not dedicated, like in my day."

"St. Jerome said that, in the sixth century," Clare scolded.

"Which only goes to show what a very wise old doctor he was."

"Actually, John—" Clare tilted her head to question his

preparedness for serious talk, and received a nod. "I need a bit of wisdom."

"I'm not too well up, these days, Clare," Chesterton warned. "Funny how quick it goes."

"Not clinical. Nothing that simple."

"Oh dear. But ask away. Helen guessed there was something."

"Taunton. Olive Hanwell."

"I read he got off."

"Came back yesterday." She told the details of Taunton's plight. "He seems to have no understanding of the situation."

"Where is he now?"

"Still at the priest's house."

Chesterton glanced up at her tone but let it go for the moment. "Why did you not let Andy Greig go if he was doing night call?"

"The priest came for me. His own idea, not mine."

"Quite a nocturnal gathering."

Clare agreed wearily. "True. Everybody's having a go. The village council. The Men's Confraternity. The Village Wives. It's becoming quite a confrontation."

"Have the police been sensible?"

Clare looked away for a moment and used the pause to adjust the position of her chair so she too could look at the sea and observe the distant coloured yachts in their slow gliding dance.

"I think they have." She must have sounded too defensive because her old colleague made an avoiding gesture.

"All right, Clare. I wasn't prying."

"Sorry, John. I'm on edge."

The old man watched Clare attentively while she recounted the events. So much of what had happened seemed to involve the priest, to hear her tell it.

"You see, John," she concluded, "that priest seems unable to make a definite response to anything. He's so *ineffectual*. A real non-person, a complete non-event." She pulled herself in. "As for Mrs. Winner—"

"*Hilda* Winner? Next door to Taunton?"

"Yes. Apparently Taunton went for his blessed cat. Mrs. Winner seems to have panicked, slammed the door. The lads were there and heard—made matters worse."

"That'll be old Stan Deller fuelling the fire," Chesterton observed.

"Or Hilda Winner herself."

Chesterton shook his head. "No. Old Deller. Sure as God made apples. I always suspected the old devil of having his eye on Hilda."

"Nothing wrong with that, surely?" Clare said a little sharply.

"It's fair enough." Chesterton was amused, but watching Clare. "So what's the problem?"

"It's going bad."

"What exactly?"

"The sense of it. The village is split into groups, John. I don't like it."

"All right, Clare. The militia's one group. Who is in the other?"

"I don't know. I suppose George Falconer—"

"Not George." Chesterton was laughing. "He's a real Vicar of Bray. You ask Sarah Horn—and we both know which group she's in. She'll tell you George is her greatest ally."

"But he's so reasonable—"

"To everyone. He's a chameleon, the village's only politician."

"Well, Ed Edgeworth."

"One," John Chesterton counted. "But he's a teacher, remember. A vulnerable position."

"I suppose," she said reluctantly, "Reverend Watson."

"Two. Is that all?"

"Possibly Nurse Batsford. I'm not sure."

The old doctor ignored her tone. "And you, Clare?"

Her answer came sudden and hot. "I'm in no group, John. A doctor can't take sides."

"A doctor always *has* to, Clare," he said gently. "And often with no chance of altering any side's aims."

"I hate the thought of siding with that . . . bumbler."

"It's obvious," he said drily. "But you'll be more pleased at Edgeworth's presence in your camp, I take it."

"What's that supposed to mean?" she demanded indignantly.

"Nothing, nothing."

"John. Tell me two things. Before Helen comes with tea. First: have I got this wretched priest completely wrong? I mean, you knew him for a short time before I arrived in Beckholt."

"Wrong? I can't see him like you see him, Clare. That's for sure. But if you're asking is he obstructive and useless, as you seem to suggest, the answer is, Yes, you've got him completely wrong, by my reckoning."

"But he's a fool, John. He's so naïve. He's . . . exasperating."

"If that's the worst mankind ever becomes, we'll not do badly."

"And as for any *sense!*" she exploded, angry at her old colleague's air of reason, "he's a laughing-stock. Any of his so-called parishioners can con him without lifting a finger. You wouldn't believe how gullible the man is! There's Jane Lang, playing her old game—"

"Next."

"I beg your pardon?"

"Next. You had two questions, Clare."

She forced herself to calm down. "It's the . . . militia, really, John." She leaned forward. "How far will they go?"

"Against Taunton?" He was deadly serious. "A great deal further than last night, Clare."

"But . . . the law. And the villagers have grown up together. Like one big family. And Taunton's one of them."

"And you called the Reverend Watson naïve?" He smiled to neutralize the riposte.

"That's not fair, John!"

"Pax, pax, love. All I mean is, do you know any hatred worse than a family feud?"

She shivered, chastened. He asked her if she would rather go indoors. She refused with thanks. The day was still quite warm and the wind had died about midday.

Helen poked her head from the window behind them.

"Wind up your medical rubbish, you two," she called cheerfully. "Coming, ready or not."

"She means she'll be out in two minutes," John Chesterton confided with a smile, as if his wife had given a well-concealed hint. "Will you take advice, Clare?" he asked benevolently, and continued on her agreement, "Wars make for strange allies. A doctor can only stand firm on his own personal convictions, and they begin where his medical knowledge ends."

"John. A doctor's the *opposite* of a priest."

"Your generation says that, Clare. Mine thinks they're the same thing."

"Nonsense. We help to rid people of superstitious delusions!"

"Let's agree to differ. But you may need his help."

"Help? From a priest?"

"To keep Taunton alive."

Clare blanched and breathed, "That bad, John?"

"That bad."

"But I'm there to make people well, mend them," she cried in distress.

"No, Clare. I'm afraid you represent more than that."

"Prove it, John."

"Easy." He was maddeningly unperturbed. "Hide for two days."

"*Hide?*"

"Do your job, hold surgeries, do it all. But stay indoors, never let yourself be seen around the village by anyone."

"What's the good of that?"

"It'll prove my point. By the end of the second day the whole village will be calling in on some pretext or other, or walking past your garden, phoning Jackie Hughes at home for no reason at all. They're like children, you see. They'll want reassurance you're still there." Chesterton smiled reflectively. "But don't tell Jackie Hughes it was my suggestion if you actually *do* try it out. She'll get on at me."

"But you make it sound . . . black magic."

"True. But babies do it all the time, don't they? Just testing the universe, making sure everything's in it's proper place out there. Call it black magic, primitive, infantile, mediaeval, anything you like. It's only everything mankind is."

"People aren't that weak," Clare cried.

"Don't be stubborn," he said pleasantly. "Or you'll not get any fat-free scones."

"Break!" Helen cried, emerging with a loaded tray. "Pull that table out, John."

Clare decided to enjoy the Chestertons' witty conversation for the next few minutes, but took the opportunity of Helen's rearranging to whisper to John without letting his wife overhear, "John, before I go tell me Taunton's and Deller's medical histories. Okay?"

"Okay," he whispered back theatrically. "Lost the envelopes?"

"No."

"Okay. It's a deal."

"If that whispering is medical or sex," Helen said sweetly, "I promise to let you both *starve*. But if it's gossip, tell *me*."

"Sorry, Helen," Clare said contritely.

"How's Mrs. Davidson at Hall Farm?" John Chesterton prompted.

"Oh, just the same as ever," Clare said on cue. "Except that Bertie's started gambling her money—"

"Really?" Helen squeaked excitedly. "Wait till we get seated, then we can relish every word!"

At half-time Beckholt was losing two-nil. A disputed free kick had precipitated a fight on the pitch. The referee, already apprehensive by the start, was flustered enough to speak harshly to both captains during the tempestuous first half. Each captain said, "Right, ref," but stared stonily at the other throughout his stern lecture. Two spectators fought briefly when the second Fieldham goal was awarded but were separated by the bystanders. Nobody joked during the break. Both teams stood apart, hardly speaking even amongst themselves, and waited for the whistle to restart the game.

CHAPTER 16

Les Taunton's smile faded at the sight of his cottage. Its overgrown appearance was worsened by the daylight. Somehow he had expected to see it as he had left it, fairly tidy and with the narrow path cut away, the grass cut to a reasonable length.

Added to its unkempt state, the thatch was charred at the right front corner where the lads had fired it. Lucky the rain stopped that before it got too much hold. The windows were smashed, each of the small square panes broken in with one exception. It would cost a fortune to mend, glass being the price it was. And putty. And new hinges for the door, and maybe new doors front and back.

He walked round the path. The hedges were dense, straggling, showing a flattened recess where he scrabbled to escape into Hilda Winner's garden and thence into the adjoining playing fields. His apple-trees were unmolested, but somebody more thorough than the rest had kicked in his wooden water-butt and hauled a pipe off the wall. All the rear windows were broken. One window-frame was hanging free, its sash weight in the grass below. The kitchen door was gone, hurled across the garden and lying partly hidden in the tall grass.

He sat on the front step trying to feel that he'd actually come home. It was too difficult and soon he gave it up. There was too much newness, too close a sense of being a stranger. Yet he had been born in that cottage near the Miskells' labourer's cottage where the footpath wound down towards Saints Brook. He had been to school in the village, worked here all his life. Other people could be treated as incomers—and some of the villagers had given many incomers a right royal welcome, in the wrong sense of the words—but not he. Not Les Taunton. Surely not he? Well, his mam had moved away, gone into Colnebridge to be near Uncle Ted now they were both getting on, but that was the sort of thing elderly folk did. Even that didn't make him an incomer, not by a mile.

A voice called through the hedge. "Is that you, Les?"

"Yes, Mrs. Winner."

"I'll bring some groceries round. What would you need?"

"Some electric."

Her voice sounded smiling. "I can't basket that round to you, silly. You eaten?"

"Had some chips at the Reverend's."

"When?"

"Dinner-time."

"Is that all?" Disapproval now. "Come round. I've baked, and just as well, it seems."

"Is it all right?"

"Tea in ten minutes."

That tone of voice was incontestable. He rose and crunched in on the glass shreds. His case had been kicked open and his clothes scattered. Three shirts and his spare trousers were outside, still wet from the rain. His underpants and ties were stuffed in the lavatory pan. The sink was filled almost to overflowing but somebody had turned the water off at the main's stopcock under the kitchen cupboard. Presumably Joe Sheldon had gone round trying to minimize the damage. The kitchen floor and hallway were spread with mud. A clod of grassy earth was wedged in the meat safe. Earth was everywhere, small stones and thrown gravel. The bulbs were shattered in every room and the radio was a crushed heap against one wall.

His bed was a profusion of flocks and feathers where the pillows and mattress had been slit. It was a frozen picture of violence, a crazy demented explosion of berserk fury directed against himself. But surely violence of this degree was only possible against an unknown person, like the Germans were unknown on the other side of No-Man's-Land. Only incomers provoked this kind of rage. How come, then, it had been accidentally turned, so wrongly and so bewilderingly, against himself? Something here was impossible, like a dream which, even while dreaming, you know is a clear impossibility and therefore must be a dream. But the lads had pissed on his ruined bed and smashed every cup and saucer and plate in the cottage.

It wasn't a joke. It wasn't a drunken spree.

He wondered who to ask. He was going to have a bite with Mrs. Winner. She would say something, but women were often very funny about houses being in a mess. Maybe he'd best say nothing. She might give him a hell of a rollicking and blame him. Better wait, he decided, pretend everything was just as he left it, keep mum. That'd give him time to sweep up and clear some of the worst mess away. Though rain always drove against his front windows this time of year. Plastic? He could borrow plastic, tack it over the gaps. If they'd left the hammer and the tacks.

Dr. Salford hadn't been nice last night. For some reason she hadn't liked him being at the priest's house. And she'd told the priest off, in that sly way women sometimes did, looking the same as usual but mad underneath, so you knew that if you weren't there to overhear she'd have come right out with it and given poor old Reverend a drubbing. Sergeant Sheldon had exchanged words with Reverend, but more open, like. Though he too had been edgy and kept trying to shout questions, same as that fat man in the court all those endless and useless weeks before they let him come home to a village that had changed, a village where all the lads seemed to think that sitting in that curved wooden stall for so long had changed him—Les Taunton for heaven's sake—from a Beckholtian to an incomer.

The Reverend, now, *was* an incomer, definitely. But he was the sort who knew straight off how wrong things could be. You could tell that as soon as you met him, though he couldn't tell people off like old Rector Colinson could, breathing hellfire dawn till dusk. Reverend Watson had a hard time putting words together, same as he himself had, even though it was said he had letters after his name and was a great non-stop reader, four books a week from the library van regular as clockwork.

He sighed. Best get round to Mrs. Winner's and eat her bake or she'd get mad for him being late. He was hungry. He had a brainwave and struggled the front door to, scraping the broken glass aside with his shoe to accomplish it. That way, Mrs. Winner might not see the mess if she passed along the lane.

"Les Taunton."

"Yes, Mrs. Winner?"

"Are you coming or not?"

"Yes, Mrs. Winner."

"Then come, slowcoach."

He hurried obediently down his overgrown path. A distant shout reminded him. Of course, the match would be ending about now. It gave him the notion of calling in the pub and having a pint with the lads. Talk things over.

Beckholt lost three-nil. They walked from the muddy field in deep silence. None raised a word in reply to the jeers and catcalls of the Fieldham people. A Beckholt girl clawed at a Fieldham girl. Their friends pulled them apart, spitting and scratching.

When the Fieldham players emerged, delighted at their success, every tyre of their waiting cars had been let down. A drizzle began. Six windscreens in the Beckholt cars were smashed by flints and car jacks. Fights broke out amid shouted recriminations. Somebody in the social club telephoned Sergeant Sheldon, who arrived to find everything apparently quiet and ordered.

He stood by until the Fieldham people had inflated their tyres and departed.

Ed found the priest battling with the undergrowth alongside the churchyard. The inevitable gang of schoolchildren accompanied him, jumping and shouting as they came. Where they came from, each time the teacher went abroad, amazed and delighted Shaw. It was as if they had some extraordinary inbuilt communication system, very like the hovering birds who showed the rest of the flock where seeds were being sown and could thus bring scores within moments.

"Has your mob brought their shears?" he joked, pausing breathlessly.

"Any of you going to help Reverend?" Ed bawled at the children.

"Can't! We're busy."

"You're out of luck, Reverend," the teacher grinned.

"See you, Mr. Edgeworth!"

"Catch one for me," the teacher shouted after the departing crowd. "Salmon!"

"You'll be lucky!"

The priest wiped his forehead and ran his handkerchief round his collar. Ed eyed the long ditch. Two hundred feet, along the roadside.

"Who helps with this?" he asked with curiosity.

"Well, nobody, really." The priest grinned. "Keeps me thin."

"I thought Eric Carnforth's mob did it."

"The Men's Confraternity?" Embarrassment showed. "Er—I think that was the general idea."

"Chivvy them up, Shaw. Put the boot in!"

"I . . . I'm a bit embarrassed."

"I would."

"That's the trouble," Shaw said wryly. "*Everybody* else would. Cup of coffee?"

"Thought you'd never ask!"

"I'll leave my trusty billhook," Shaw decided, "or I might lack resolution to come out again."

They walked across to the rectory, waving to Col's milk-float which rattled past on its way to be batteried up at the garage, and chatting of the battle against the Fieldham footballers. Neither thought much to the harrowing tales of defeats and fights. "About par," Ed commented, seeing little significance. Indoors, the teacher said he'd make the coffee while Shaw scrubbed the rest of Beckholt off his filthy hands.

"Besides," he ribbed him, "I remember some unspeakable liquid you gave me once before. Even I couldn't do worse."

"Insult on insult!"

Using the nailbrush on his soapy hands in the bathroom, Shaw worried about their rather strained jocularity. Normally, but what exactly was "normality" any more in this village?— normally, he and Ed were almost at ease with one another, though they actually met very little. Since the big reorganization, of course, the primary school no longer counted as a Church foundation. Everything in these modern days came under the local education authority. Indeed, it was this change to the new scheme which had enabled the headmistress, Mrs. James, to employ another teacher, that being Ed. Inevitably there were rumours, that Mrs. James knew Ed in the past, perhaps in their university days. And, as so often happens, circumstance compounded rumour—Mrs. James was of an age with Ed, and her husband was said to be one of those travellers forever selling building materials in the Midlands. Naturally the village talked, a youngish woman with a practically mythical husband and a handsome young teacher . . .

He went downstairs slightly depressed. Was it an omen that, within seconds of Ed's running into him, the teacher was already on at him for being too reticent, too facile? So many people seemed to share Ed's attitude—Clare Salford first and most, by that prettified aggression which was so unnerving; then Esther Batsford, but of course in a milder, friendlier way without that terrifying steel.

"Best you've ever tasted, Shaw. You see!"

"Thanks. Sorry about the mitts."

Ed glanced towards the priest's hands. "A good attempt, but you'll have difficulty cleaning those nails before Communion, Shaw."

"I soak them. Esther—er, Nurse Batsford—showed me. There's a bottle of green stuff somewhere."

Ed had laid the tray in the parlour, having filched the remaining biscuits and spread them on a plate. He looked up candidly. "Was Esther the little leprechaun who cleaned the kitchen? It's glittering in there. Sugar?"

Shaw reddened, tried to nod casually. "She came in to see to Taunton."

"What does *she* think about Taunton, Shaw? Your side or theirs?"

Shaw responded swiftly. "Side? I keep saying there are no *sides*, Ed. It's not a match."

"Everybody else says there are two."

"Who's everybody?"

"The opposition." Ed laughed at the tautology. "Sarah the vigilante. Eric Carnforth and his merry men. The village council. All those silly buggers—sorry, Shaw, forget we're in the rectory for a minute—who signed that imbecilic petition."

"What are they actually opposing, Ed?"

"Taunton's return."

"And *who* are they against?"

"Anybody who supports Taunton's return." Ed crunched a biscuit and spooned sugar into his own cup.

"That means against the entire nation's law, Ed. It's crazy."

"Are you sure it's as crazy as all that?"

"Certainly!" In his agitation Shaw rose and paced the carpet. "Look, Ed. It's a simple matter of acceptance. Taunton's back in his cottage right now, getting on with life—"

"Is he?" the teacher interrupted, surprised.

"Yes. And what has that got to do with anyone in the village? He has the sanction of society, its legal permission, to go home and pick up the threads." The priest flapped his hands in exasperation. "It'll die down, this . . . this fear, this stupid reaction."

"Are you sure of that, Shaw?" Ed asked quietly.

Shaw froze. "Aren't you, Ed?"

"Afraid not. I talked with George, Eric, the Joneses."

Shaw soberly returned to his chair. "Have you any reasons, Ed? Don't," he put in quickly before Ed could reply, "don't give me any hunches. I'm sick of guesses, people having vague superstitious ideas."

"Shaw. Taunton's in danger. It's that serious."

"I know it's serious! But *reasons*, Ed."

"You forget what I am. I'm a teacher, Shaw. I have access to a unique source of information which, rightly or wrongly, is tapped from virtually every household in the village."

Light dawned on Shaw. "The children?"

Ed nodded. "I realize it's highly privileged knowledge. But without even trying I learn what people eat, how often they fight, when—and how—they have sexual intercourse and with whom, who likes whom. And," he concluded evenly, "who hates."

"In class, what they say at playtime, things like that?"

"Mostly. Those are the most obvious ways. But there's also a sort of—well, I can only call it a kind of osmosis. They behave differently. There's something furtive crept into them."

The priest remembered the children in the lane a moment ago. "They didn't look very furtive."

"I'm not talking about mere behaviour."

"But Taunton's only been back since—"

"Correct, Shaw. And I've spoken to a good half of my own class. They shout football scores as they pass, bring a lettuce from their gardens, call in groups on some pretext or other, walk with me when I go to the shop."

The priest grimaced inwardly. It was a wonderful pipedream, the kind of image he had once dreamed for himself, when finally he would have his own parish. Was a priest basically unapproachable? Or was it only himself, something fundamentally cold or wrong in his emotional make-up?

"What do your . . . contacts tell you?"

"That Taunton is in real danger. Of his life."

Shaw thought a minute, trying out the strangeness of the idea. "From whom?"

"The villagers."

"I don't believe that. The police, Ed. You should go to Joe Sheldon."

The teacher avoided Shaw's eyes, the first sign of wavering Ed had ever displayed.

"That's what I came about. I can't."

"Why not? You've seen him often enough lately."

Ed smiled ruefully. "Heard about our joyous gathering at the White Hart, eh?" He shrugged, suddenly looking tired and drawn. "I want you to go, Shaw."

"Me? And say what?"

"Just pass the word. Say you've heard on the grapevine—"

"How can I? He'd ask where I picked such a story up. He'd want chapter and verse. You know what Joe's like."

"That's exactly it. I'd lose the children's trust if I went about disclosing confidences."

"But you wouldn't be 'disclosing,' Ed. It's confidential."

Ed laughed, a harsh croak. "In this village? You know you're talking rubbish."

"But it's—"

"Don't tell me it's my responsibility, Shaw, for goodness sake. It's not. It's our side's *collective* responsibility, not mine alone. I've thought it all out."

"In a very confused way, if I may say so." The priest's cup was empty. He gazed unhappily into it. "I'm sorry, Ed. But it is your duty."

"It's *ours*, Shaw! Yours and mine and Clare Salford's."

"I never said it's yours alone, Ed." Shaw realized that he was speaking with something like dignity. "And I'm not so sure about Dr. Salford, not knowing quite where she stands. But it's mine. I accept that. And it's yours."

The teacher was relieved. "So you'll pass word along to Joe?"

"Of course—if you won't."

"Say you just heard." Ed became enthusiastic. "No need to say how—"

"I shall have to, Ed. Joe Sheldon takes little notice of me."

Ed banged his knee. "No, Shaw. Can't you see? The children would never trust me again. My life would be a misery. You've no idea how vicious kids can be. They'd think of it as betrayal, especially if Joe came questioning . . . No." He was emphatic. "No, Shaw. You can't."

"I can. You ought. And if you don't I'll have to."

"Look, Shaw." Ed rose, red-faced and angry. "I came here in good faith, wanting to protect this bloke Taunton. I didn't expect to be told to ruin my job. It's bloody difficult building up a relationship with children, especially in teaching. It's all right for you, without a proper daily responsibility. A priest has it made. Well, a teacher doesn't. He has to slog his way in, gaining trust inch by inch. I know because I've done it. And I'll tell you one thing, *Reverend*—I'm not going to have it fouled up by you or anybody else."

"I'm sorry, but—" He could only see his fingers with their in-

grained dirt and the empty cup. His ears and face were reddening with shame.

"Don't give me your regrets!" The teacher swallowed, fought
for control. "You just go along and tell Sheldon you've heard a
rumour. Tell him it's a confidential tip-off."

"He won't know how to assess its importance," Shaw said
doggedly. "Unless he's told the source he'll ignore any warning."

"Very well," Ed said tightly. "Sheldon'll have to do the best
he can without any tip-off."

"No, Ed." Shaw rose wearily to face the teacher. "It's either
duty or no duty. I think it's duty."

"So you and your fucking duty are going to ruin my position
here!" Ed shouted. "Is that it?"

"That's a secondary issue—"

"Oh, is it!" The teacher tapped Shaw's chest, suddenly vicious
and quiet. "It might look secondary from where you're sitting,
Reverend, but it's primary to me. You have a cushy number,
and no problems except those you decide you'll invent. For you
it's a doddle. Well, it's time you realized that the rest of us have
a life full of problems you've never dreamed of, and couldn't
hope to understand. And they're not problems we chose to pick
up because we're bored sick! They're pushed on us day in and
day out because we live out there in a real hard world, where
we have to graft for our wages!"

"Listen. Please."

"No, Reverend." Edgeworth halted, too furious for coher-
ence. "You listen. Tell tales to Sheldon and I'll disclaim it. And
I'll see that word spreads among the kids. *Then* see how far
your bloody hocus-pocus gets you on Sundays."

"Ed—"

But the teacher had slammed out. Shaw hesitated. Should
he run out, try to walk with him, somehow persuade Ed to cool
down and discuss the matter soberly? He sat dismally. Was
there some felicitous phrase, an elegant quip to suit the occasion?
If so, why had he not managed to find it ready on his tongue?
And, final carping whine, why had the seminary authorities
not taught it to him, drilled an eager young priest in the proper

therapy for such an agitated man? Training. A priest should be *trained*, not ordained. But possibly therapy was out there nowadays, in Ed's real and problematic world, and nothing to do with a mere hocus-pocus man. And possibly even less to do with a man of God—if indeed he was that.

He stayed seated. The day was drawing in. His gardening tools were still out by the graveyard hedge. He ought to do a bit more out there, at least, while there was usable daylight. But first he'd have to contact Sergeant Sheldon and explain about Taunton's danger. Of course, the fear was absurd. People like these villagers couldn't possibly injure one of their own.

Presumably that was why Ed was so distraught—by his efforts and extrovert nature he had removed the incomer's stigma from himself. Original sin, perhaps, an accidental original sin of being born elsewhere, by which a person was condemned untried and unheard.

Wearily he went out to the hall. He dithered at the telephone, hoping Sheldon might not answer even if he did dare ring. There was the hedge to get on with, Sheldon to dial, supper to put on, the parish accounts to do for the next meeting. It was giving him a headache.

"Hello? Mrs. Sheldon?" He must have dialled mechanically, without conscious thought.

"Yes. That you, Reverend?"

"Er, yes. Is—er—Joe free for a second, please?"

CHAPTER 17

Les was leaving his neighbour's cottage.

"Thanks, Mrs. Winner."

"You're welcome."

"And thanks for the groceries."

"Get on with you. Got Hawkeyes?"

"Yes, thanks, Mrs. Winner."

"If you need anything come round."

He went off carrying the bag she'd given him and holding Hawkeyes. Dusk lay on the evening air as Hilda closed the door. She went to sit for a moment at the table.

He'd eaten well, made a good meal, really appreciated every mouthful. Odd how satisfying it was to a woman, having a good bake and making a substantial spread which was then gone in less than an hour once a hungry man got his feet under the table.

She'd spent more time watching him than eating herself. He had talked without reticence, even enthusiastically, giving an account of his confinement and the trial, how people had reacted. His view of life was curiously untroubled. Every hour simply came in its turn and went. For Les there didn't seem sense in connecting hours together. His was the outlook of an elementary man, an unthought and perhaps even daft approach to life, but was it entirely ridiculous just because it wasn't her own? He had failed to understand even the simplest questions, often jumping to conclusions and frequently having to ask what a word meant.

Yet his perception was often acute. His alarmingly candid summary of Dr. Salford: *She wants you to think she doesn't bother about Reverend.* And his equally outspoken comment on the priest: *If I was clever like him I wouldn't be scared as him.* And when she'd asked about his stay at the rectory—only to help him gain confidence by getting him to talk more—he had shown an uncanny awareness of the damaging possibilities where the priest was concerned: *That Nurse Batsford likes Reverend but you can't tell anybody because he'll have to work out what folk thought.*

He'd avoided mentioning the terrible state of the cottage. Quite like a child telling its first lie, unbelievably clumsy yet hoping its painfully transparent subterfuge was passing undetected. She smiled, remembering his fiction as he described his pleasure at seeing his familiar things, and after the meal he'd played with the black-and-white cat. Hawkeyes had welcomed him casually, accepting his return as a tribute and letting him feed her.

Now he'd gone next door the room seemed empty. She had forgotten how a man fills a room, extends his presence in some unfathomable way into the corners and out into other rooms until the whole place alters by his presence. Now that presence was gone the cottage was settling into its old blank habit. She reached across and touched the knife he'd used. She lifted his cup and ran a finger along the rim, smiling at the moist crumb which had lodged there. He was certainly a rough diamond, not one of your high intellects. But did these things matter? Simple, yet dreamy. And who would have thought that he loved the radio so fervently? For during the meal he had cried out excitedly that a music programme was on one of the wavelengths, apparently a regular programme she'd never heard of. The only broadcasts she ever bothered with were the housewife's hour morning and afternoon and those early friendlies with light music interspersed with a bit of humour. She'd had to give him the radio and he'd tuned it quick as that. The music wasn't her cup of tea but he went into raptures, telling who composed it and knowing the name of every instrument playing. He was so carried away that once, as she buttered him more bread, he failed to reply. She'd looked up and caught his eyes glazed, completely blank, so wrapped up was he in the music. Twice she'd had to repeat the question, smiling at her recollection of his coming to when the small transistor radio crackled. Probably her question showed such a hopeless ignorance of serious music it wasn't worth answering. More than likely.

She *had* been worried. She admitted it frankly to herself. I mean, an accused man, though now sent home free. It had taken courage . . . or perhaps her own need had overridden natural caution? Anyway, her fear was real. And she certainly had watched him. She sat on, looking at the uncleared table.

When Eric Carnforth and George Falconer were shown in by Sandra, Mrs. Davidson was talking to Bertie over a glass of wine. She waved them in, telling them to "find a parking space." Ber-

tie instantly said he'd better be seeing to the tractors for tomorrow and with a friendly nod to the visitors left the room.

Joan Davidson was amused at his departure. Nobody in the
village could possibly be ignorant of his precise role in her
household, but Bertie insisted on this ritualistic subservience
whenever anyone called. She noted in passing that Bertie had
carefully closed the double door which led into her spacious
hall, signifying that, although he could just as easily have left
by the french windows, he was probably now going to enter the
central farmyard via the kitchen and its garden. Which meant,
she observed relentlessly, smiling affably at her visitors, that Bertie and Sandra would be together in the kitchen for as long as
they liked while she had this useless pair to entertain. Nothing
for it, she told herself. Sandra, all seventeen years and 36D cups
of her, would have to go—like the pneumatic Betty and that
bouncy Frances before her. She was slightly tipsy. The homemade wine had been a mistake. If only she had known these
crumbs were on their way—

"Would you have a glass? I'm just having one."

George drew breath but to his chagrin Eric said no for them
both.

"We'd better ask you straight out, Mrs. Davidson."

"Why Eric Carnforth!" she giggled, watching his discomfiture.

"Please, Mrs. Davidson, it's a serious matter."

"I'll behave. It's about Taunton, isn't it?"

"Yes." Eric glanced at George for support. One never knew
quite how much Joan Davidson got to know about the village's
goings-on. Way out here, down on the Saints Brook practically
hidden by woods with the marshy ground in the valley bottoms
preventing any access from the south, you tended to assume she
was cut off from Beckholt, though of course there was always
the footpath leading into the old church ruins which showed in
the thickets from times before the land sank in the 1880s. It
was all her land until Colnebridge began. And in any case folk
were rather wary of Joan Davidson. Scandal tended to protect
her as much as the village's topography.

"He's back," George contributed.

"There was some disturbance, I heard."

"Some," George agreed. "But it's over now."

"But he's gone to his cottage," Eric informed her. "Shows every sign of staying."

"Well?" Mrs. Davidson spoke brightly into the pause.

"Well." Eric cleared his throat. "It rather puts the ball in our court. Him being here, acting as if nothing's wrong."

"And is there?" She waited, prompted, "Anything wrong?"

"Well, isn't there? A man like him?"

"I hardly know him, so how could I know?"

She crossed her legs as casually as she could manage. Eric's eyes wobbled, then determinedly fixed on the middle distance. George, the old rascal, was delighted by the flash of leg. He'd been a devil in his day, but of course she'd been so preoccupied with opportunities a lot younger than he . . .

"We have a petition, Mrs. Davidson. Representing the wishes of the village."

"That Taunton should be hanged anyway?" Her mischief displeased Carnforth, but she could see George was enjoying the visit.

"Of course not. But the feeling is strongly that he should be encouraged to leave."

"Run out of town?" She clapped her hands eagerly. "Like out west?"

"No, not that."

"Then what? Does your petition have a plan?"

"Not really." Eric's glance at George met with no response. Why, the Falconer man was practically ogling her. And she was doing little to discourage his attention. "It's been left to . . . to the council chairman," he informed her, smiling grimly to himself. It wasn't all going to be left to him. He'd make sure of that.

Mrs. Davidson looked into George's eyes. "And you've decided *what* exactly?"

"Er, oh." He was momentarily flustered. "Er . . ."

"The jobs," Eric reminded him with satisfaction.

"Yes. Taunton worked at Terry's garage before the arrest." George got back on track. "And he helped Bert—er—he helped you in Hall Farm, I believe."

"Yes. I think he did a few days."

George reluctantly bit the bullet. "We heard he worked here every week." He tried unsuccessfully to form it into a question, to Eric's evident annoyance.

"We are informed one day, two evenings, Mrs. Davidson."

She smiled. She hated cold fish. She deliberately sweetened her voice. "And how could your information be erroneous, Mr. Carnforth?"

"Saturdays and the evenings which your, um, foreman decided."

She raised her eyebrows in polite interest, thinking, I'd rather have a murderer sitting there on my best chintz than you nigglers. Neither of them looked as if they ever sweated or spat. Synthetic dextrose for blood. Hadn't they heard that Man was animal?

"And was his labour to my satisfaction?"

Eric shuffled uncomfortably. This was getting out of hand. "Only you . . . your staff can say that, Mrs. Davidson."

"And I take it you are here to notify his readiness to resume this part-time work."

"Resume . . . ?"

"Why, yes." Her wide eyes were completely innocent.

Eric was confused. "Er, George?" The amused woman sipped her wine, straight-faced.

George cleared his throat. "It's like this. The village wants him, well, *not* to start work again."

"And go on the dole?"

"Not that. Just . . . remain unemployed."

Eric resumed, "The village wants him barred, Mrs. Davidson."

"I see. Isn't that rather extreme?"

"It is. But so is murder."

"Whom did he murder, Mr. Carnforth?"

His lips thinned. "We all know that, Mrs. Davidson."

"Then please inform me," she cooed. "So we can send for that delicious Inspector Young in Colnebridge and he can arrest the wretched man."

"That's already been done, as you well know."

"Have you discussed this with Bertie?"

"Bertie?" Carnforth echoed with alarm.

"My foreman," Joan Davidson smiled. "Surely you've met him? He was here a moment ago. Let me send—"

"Thank you. That won't be necessary." George rose, signalling to Eric with a nod. "We'd better get along."

"Do you mean you refuse to come into line with the village, Mrs. Davidson?"

"Let me think." She posed prettily, crossing her legs again and leaning forward in the traditional pose of the thinker. "Yes," she said after a moment, pleasant still. "Yes, I believe I mean exactly that."

"And you'll accept this . . . criminal murderer on to your farm?"

She made a wide-eyed stare of mock horror. "And be murdered in my *bed*? Mind your own business."

"I take that to mean you will."

"Take it any way you bloody well please," she said sweetly.

"Then you won't mind if I report your transgression back to my committee!" Carnforth said waspishly.

"Eric," George tried warningly.

"If you've nothing better to do," Joan Davidson said.

"I'll report their decision to you in writing!"

"Big deal."

"And you can take the consequences! Your farm depends on Beckholt, just remember that!"

"We'd better go, Mrs. Davidson," George said apologetically and making for the door.

"You better had," the reclining woman agreed mildly.

She waited till they were almost out into the hall before speaking.

"Mr. Carnforth."

"Yes?" The man turned, white with anger.

"You're a *bore*," she said evenly. "Such a bloody *bore*."

The door closed.

CHAPTER 18

Ken Young replaced the receiver and sent for Detective-Sergeant Hawksmoor. He was searching the Taunton files when his deputy came in.

"Don't say it, Ken," Hawksmoor said.

"I bloody well will. What's going on out there, for Christ's sake?"

"I heard what Sergeant Sheldon's reported."

"Didn't we all? It's queer as a clockwork orange." He swore inelegantly for a few seconds and buzzed for coffee.

"Sheldon's no slouch, Ken."

"Don't you start, Charlie, for Gawd's sake," the inspector said disgustedly. "What we want are fewer warnings. The bloody skies're full of portents, magpies, weird and wonderful omens. Know how I feel, Charlie? Like the sound's gone off in the middle of a radio commentary in the England-Scotland match. You know everything's continuing, yet you know sod all."

The inspector studied Hawksmoor for a moment.

"You were on the Taunton case."

"For my sins. It seemed cut and dried." Ken's words earlier, to Clare at the cottage.

"They're the worst."

"You've got my excellent incisive reports on it, I see."

"This crap?" Ken Young turned the files over with a finger as if they were contaminated. "You know as well as I do they're only the cosy chat, the gloss."

"Ta, Sybil." Hawksmoor accepted the coffee and waited until the woman had left. "There'll be no bloody sugar in it. Sure as eggs." He sipped, grimaced. "See? Good detective work, that. Try yours."

Ken shook his head, joked absently. "I'm not daft. This bloke."

"Taunton? Born slow, a clodhopper if you ask me, Ken. Not the world's brightest. No record. Mother lives in Colnebridge. Born and bred in the village. One of nature's innocents, until he murdered that lass."

"Did he?" the inspector asked soberly.

"Do it?" Charlie Hawksmoor thought a long time before answering. "You know, Ken, I rather think he didn't."

"But you concluded the opposite in this."

"The party line, Ken." Hawksmoor gave a Gallic shrug. "Evidence speaks louder than words sometimes. Especially in the early stages of the investigation."

"And the opposite happens."

"But that doesn't call for rushing out into the village and lining them up against the wall, starting the whole bloody thing over again."

"Sheldon says there's a report of crime, Charlie. *Crime.* Coming our way.

"He'll be right, Ken."

"I know that, you silly sod." The senior spoke without rancour. "But *why?*"

Charlie guffawed. "Going sociological, Ken? The unending search for motive?" He gave a derisory snort. "As if motive ever mattered, in anything. People are what they do. We're the sum total of all our actions. Thoughts are irrelevant, especially in crime."

"Then what action do we take for the protection of loyal subjects going about their innocent lives in this bloody village?"

"Go and see that schoolmaster?"

"I will," the inspector said.

"You?"

"Me. But first I'll see this priest."

"They're all practically new. None of them knew Taunton."

"All the better. Maybe I'll get an objective viewpoint."

Charlie Hawksmoor did not miss the sarcasm in the chief's voice, and was still laughing as Ken buzzed for an official car.

Les Taunton thumbed down the Suffolk latch of the Queen's Head taproom and entered the smoke and hubbub, grinning in anticipation at the way the lads would react.

The juke-box was going, the darts team practising for a pint every three games, 501 up to double finish as always, and two old blokes were trying to do down old Robertson at shove ha'penny, though nobody had ever yet got the better of the old violin-maker's steady hands. Jenny was serving. She looked up in amazement. Les chuckled at her expression, pushing through the crowd, nodding and smiling. A few muttered greetings came in return, but they all seemed a bit startled at his arrival. His grin became fixed, but still showed frank pleasure.

"Evening, Frank, Bob."

"Hello."

"Hello, Del." Les nodded down the short arm of the bar counter to where Del was staring at him.

"Hello, Les." Del finished drawing the pint for Dusty Lang and took the money. "You're back, then."

Les chuckled. "I'm no ghost, Del. Pint, please."

Jenny darted a silent question towards Del before drawing the bitter. Les liked a mug in the old fashion, though he never affected a silver one of his own to hang behind the bar the way some youngsters did nowadays.

"Hello, Jenny. Busy as ever?"

"Terrible, some days." She kept staring at him, passed the mug.

"Bet you don't grumble, eh?"

"No. Custom's always welcome."

She paid him his change and moved to serve another drinker.

The talk had died. The darts players were talking together, weighing their darts and occasionally glancing round to where Mick Robie was sitting. He was there in his favourite corner with a group of farm labourers. One's dog was slumbering under the table among their boots. Les crossed over, grinning shyly.

"Hello, Mick."

Robie lifted his eyes, gave a curt nod. "Hello, lad. You've a mind to take a drink, eh?"

"Try stopping me," Les joked.

The remark fell into the silence. He looked round to see what had happened to cause that but everything was the same as always. Almost. It was too still, quiet. People were looking-not-looking, as his grannie was wont to put it. Maybe they were a bit worried about last night's caper going wrong like it had, though that sometimes happened and he held nobody to account for it.

"We wouldn't do that, would we, Ned?"

"No." Ned was a persistent smiler, a quiet poaching man who shared a labouring job between Mrs. Davidson at the Hall Farm and Fogg Powell's busy Friday Farm.

"Would we, Dusty?"

"Not us." Dusty wasn't smiling, but Les made allowances for him. His Jane had had a miscarriage again. Mrs. Winner had told him that.

"No, Les." Mick had not shifted his eyes. "We're glad you dropped in. Especially after last night."

"No hard feelings, Mick." Les grinned shyly. It was all working out the way he'd guessed.

"That's big of you."

"Oh, I know how it is Mick. High spirits, eh?"

"That's all, Les. Isn't he right, Dusty?"

"Spot on."

"Isn't he right, Ned?"

"Dead right, Mick."

"See? We all say you're right, Les."

"Match didn't go too well today." Les kept looking for a chair but they were all taken and the bench had magically filled up. The score was on the board where the football fixtures were listed for the season.

"No. A bit of bad luck, Les."

"Three-nil, eh? Worst we've ever had, that I remember, Mick." Les looked round again into the same silence. It still wasn't quite right. They should all be talking, pulling his leg, asking him how things had been and what he'd felt like. Not to make too much of a fuss, but at least some kind of interest.

"It's as if we've got a run of bad luck, Les." Mick was piling dominoes on the table, a domino house.

"A jinx," Ned smiled.

"That's it. A jinx, Les."

"On the football team," Dusty put in, shoving a spread of dominoes over to Mick for his house building. "Couldn't be worse, could it?"

"Bad luck," Les agreed sympathetically. He knew as much as any villager what a defeat by Fieldham meant. It was as though they'd let down every single villager who had ever lived in Beckholt.

"Not just bad luck, Les." Mick balanced a domino on a cross pair of supporting pieces, holding his breath to see it in place. "Terrible."

"Still, there's another day." Les would never have said that, once. It just came out.

Mick shook his head sadly.

"You're talking like an incomer, Les. What the hell does next year matter if we've chucked the game away today?" He sat back, contemplated his domino house and resumed building sadly. "Tell me that."

"Bad luck," Les agreed. He looked round again. Nobody was speaking now. The juke-box had run out. Nobody made a move to start it up again with a coin.

"Next season's game doesn't matter a tinker's grind," Dusty said morosely.

"And why?" Mick asked. "Because it's a whole year away. That's why."

"Any villager knows that," Ned smiled.

"Then we'll wallop 'em, lads, eh?" Les grinned. His throat was dry in spite of the drink. He shouldn't have come in like that, without giving the lads warning. Maybe they were a bit embarrassed, like. After all, his name had been in all the papers. He ought to have waited a night or two.

"Pint, Ned?" Mick rose and went to the bar where Jenny served him.

Les crossed to the fixtures list, pretending to read it. The silence had grown somehow, swelled behind him. He could feel it trailing him over to the board, like leaves trail a fallen log pushed across a still pond. His shoulders prickled.

He drained his glass, trying to look easy, and put it down on Mick's table. As he did so, nervousness caused him to wobble the domino house. It tumbled, though he made an ineffectual attempt to catch most of the pieces.

"Sorry, Mick," he said. Mick was standing behind him carrying Ned's pint.

"That's all right, Les." Mick set the mug down. "Think nothing of it."

"Well, lads. I'll be off. A few things to see to at the cottage."

"So soon, Les?" Mick asked, seeming surprised. He had not gone back to his seat on the facing bench.

"Settling in, Mick. Trying to keep it in order."

"I know how it is, Les." Mick took his shoulder. "We all know how it is, don't we, Ned? Dusty? Bob? Frank?"

They all agreed they did.

"There's a pint waiting for you, Les." Mick jerked his head to indicate the bar where Jenny was drawing again. "Good health, Les."

"A pint?" Les went, warmed by the invitation. Jenny slid the mug on the counter.

"Hello again, Les. No," she stayed him, "it's paid for. Mick."

"Thanks." He looked over to Mick. "Cheers, Mick."

"Cheers, Les." The big man resumed his building, painstakingly starting on the foundations of the domino house while the others observed him without speaking.

Les was about to go over to them but Jenny asked quickly about his being away.

"Did they treat you well, Les?"

"Not bad."

"Food all right, I mean?"

"All right." He was about to turn away again but she seemed

anxious to talk now and reached over to pull his attention to her.

He started talking, then, pleased that at last the air was thinning and folk were responding to his presence. The beer was starting to freshen his mind, clear away those cobwebs of apprehension that had begun to strand round his thought the way they seemed to be doing more and more these days. A beer from Mick was a signal peace offering, and conversation from Jenny was always welcome. He started asking questions of his own within a few more minutes and Jenny kept answering, smiling eventually and nodding at every fresh subject that came up.

Eventually, too, a desultory conversation started up here and there in the taproom, which showed the lads had only been a bit embarrassed and shy for the reasons he'd already guessed. Some minutes later still the juke-box played, and when he looked round to shout Mick another pint, he noticed happily that the darts team was hard at their practice session again. But Mick was gone and Dusty and the others. In their places two old codgers were playing dominoes.

He turned away and bought Jenny one instead. She seemed more than willing and seemed relieved he wasn't going home right away. She told him she was sure he'd missed a pint in prison. He said happily that was true. He ordered another just the same.

Joan Davidson inspected her foreman with unconcealed pleasure.

"Since I sent that mousy little scrap you called your wife packing, Bertie," she said calmly, "you've been no trouble. Heavy, especially in certain positions, but not trouble."

"What's that mean?"

"Everybody keeps asking that." She held out her glass. He ignored it, refusing to submit to a mere tactic. She smiled, gratified, and swung her feet down to pour her own refill. "It means you're trouble now, dear."

"I'm not in trouble."

"Maybe. Or maybe not."

"With them two? What did they want?"

"Me to bar Taunton. Not give him a job."

"Did you agree?"

"Told them to go to hell."

The man grinned. "That's not trouble."

"Isn't it?"

"No." His grin faded. "No?"

"I've already told you it's maybe." She eyed him until he grew uncomfortable. "Olive Hanwell. The girl he's supposed to have killed."

"What about her?"

"She worked here last year. For a fortnight."

"I remember the police checking."

"Well done." She sipped, but with less enjoyment. The chill had gone from the wine, and *Spätlese* was absolute death once that happened. "Bertie. How did you find the deceased?"

"How what?"

"Good? Bad? Indifferent? I mean sexually, of course."

He stood up. "Are you bitching, or is this leading somewhere?"

"Both, dear. Sit down. Sit *down*."

He crossed to her in a swift stride, pulled her to her feet and sat down in her place, pushing her away. Her wine had spilled on the carpet. She filled the glass again carefully and went to sit in the opposite armchair. "Well?" he said patiently.

"You'll be aware of the rapid turnover in my domestic staff, Bertie."

"You do get rid of them pretty fast."

"Like I did Olive Hanwell. And for the same reason. I've never spoken of this before."

"Of *what* before?"

"You've had quite a few extras, haven't you? What with the women and girls that have served their time here—to coin a phrase."

"Don't know what you're talking about, love."

"Jane. Betty. Deirdre. That weird but alert Samantha from Aberdeen. And Olive. Many others."

He shrugged. "Where's the harm?"

"The harm is that you shagged Olive Hanwell," she answered calmly. "I don't approve, and I acknowledged that the girl was nothing less than a randy little tart without a brain in her head."

"It was a long time ago, love."

"Perhaps it's a man's proper reaction to reach out for any breast or bottom that comes into view. It seems to be yours. I simply don't know. The question is, did you keep on seeing Olive Hanwell once she was dismissed from here?"

He looked uncomfortable for the first time. "I'm not sure."

She tilted her head to examine him quizzically. "Bertie. Tell me. Does a man remember a woman every single time? I mean, you have had your share of females."

He thought. "Remember? No. Not really. Some, maybe."

"Could you with Olive Hanwell? Truth, Bertie. It's trouble for us."

"N—no, not really." He waited another second, drank absently. "I did see her once after she left."

"Once only? Where was it?"

"Here. She came to the green barn. The men were gone."

"So nobody saw you? Think, Bertie."

"No."

"Did you tell the police all this?"

"No. There was no reason to."

"How long was that before she was killed?"

"Maybe a few months. I forget."

"Silly little bitch." Joan crossed over and sat on the carpet beside his chair. "Bertie," she said eventually. "Taunton. When—if—he comes asking for his job back, give it him, will you?"

"If you say so, love."

"Yes," she said. "Definitely."

CHAPTER 19

Jenny said good night, smiling weakly at Les. He nodded to the one face turned to see him leave and headed for the door, clumsy with his feet. No aches, no worries now, only the glow of knowing he was secure among his own.

"What are you up to?" Del was grinning his fixed grin even as he hissed the question. The juke-box was giving out its last song of the night and he'd called "Time" fifteen minutes before. Most of the customers were drifting.

"Nothing." Jenny started on the glasses, polishing and calling good nights as the door latched and crashed to.

"You kept the bugger here!"

"A word does no harm."

"It can, it *has*."

"Then bar him." She called a cheerful insult to a departing labourer and received a jocular crack in return.

"Maybe I will," Del muttered. "I don't want any of this."

"Any of what?" Jenny asked innocently.

Jenny said nothing more, remembering Mick Robie's steady gaze as he'd bought a pint for Ned, then paused to lean over the counter.

"And for our hero over there, drawn slow," he'd instructed.

"For . . . ?"

"Here, Jenny love. Heard this one?" he demanded loudly, and shrouded his mutter in her ear, using his massive bulk while pretending to tell her a crude joke. "Keep him here. Half an hour at least."

"Ooooh!" she'd exclaimed, simulating offence.

"I'll see you're laid, darlin'—the going rate for the job." She felt her belly stir at the promise.

"Why?" she'd asked under her breath, knowing Del would give her what-for if she encouraged Les Taunton.

"Mind your own business, love. But even a pig won't eat a green spud."

Sickened, she'd given out her routine screech of laughter and wagged a finger in pretended scolding, telling Mick that one less like that would be an improvement.

The bar was empty now. Del was leaning on the counter gazing at nothing.

"All right, love?" she asked.

"Fine," he said, lifting himself wearily, for once looking old. "Fine."

Les was slightly bleary. The cottage needed its lights on. He could see that, even though the beer was seeing things for him. And there was smoke, more alive in the darkness, as smoke always is. Somebody lit me a fire, he wondered, but it was woodsmoke and never from a chimney. And there was a faint overlying scent in it . . .

And yet no sign of a fire, no flame. Mrs. Winner up late, her kindness driving her to greater cooking this late? But her place was in darkness too, the porch bulb out. Only the lamp down the lane shone, and a slice of moon hardly worth turning a copper over for. Old Deller's front window glowing, and himself there like a Red Indian scout on those pictures. Silence all round.

"Hawkeyes," he called, shuffling through the high grass and keeping his feet on the poor unkempt path by a countryman's trick of sliding with the weight on the toes.

The cottage was as he had left it, no more damage. Had Mrs. Winner kept an eye on it for him? She'd been kind to him since he came home, her and the priest and that Nurse Batsford, though that coloured bottle had stung worse than any nettle . . .

"Hawkeyes?"

He found his candle and lit it. More countryman's tricks to make it carryable so he could see by its help. He dropped a few wax drops to the bottom of a jam jar, sticking the bottom of the candle firmly to the waxen pool. Then he inverted a broken plant pot over it, retaining hold of it by the rim. This way, his eyes protected from the direct shine of its light, he was able to use it like a torch, seeing where he was going yet remaining undazzled by the shine.

The smoke was coming from somewhere out back. But there was nothing in the old garden worth burning. And who'd want to start a fire in his garden at this time of night? A kind neighbour is a daytimer, except for women's trouble like children and sicknesses.

He stood at the kitchen door, stepped out into the grass. A flame's last flicker showed him, led him to the bonfire. More smoke and ash remained than proper fire, though an hour ago it must have been substantial from its size.

His metal dustbin stood over the mound of embers, balanced on bricks to keep it even as the fire settled. The lid, firmly rammed down over the flanged rim, was composition and had started to melt at one side. The strange almost exotic aroma was coming from the fire and the dustbin. He knocked the dustbin off its bricks, rolled it away into the grass with a foot. The lid's handle was not hot, and he was able to haul it off by bracing a heel against the base.

He was almost retching even before he looked inside, knowing what they'd done, those pleasant mates who'd kept him talking at the pub.

Hawkeyes had tried to escape. Great shining streaks of clawed effort showed even in the dim candlelight where she'd scrabbled in terror at the interior of the metal bin as the heat and smoke increased. Now she lay on her side, smouldering and mummified, cooked. Her claws still projected, unsheathed.

Les Taunton retched and retched, letting his candle fall and stumbling away into the darker shadows of the cottage wall. He realized after a while that this was weeping. As far as he could recall he'd never wept before. Who'd have thought a funny old act like weeping could create such an ache, a dragging pain like this?

He sat and wept among the long grass and plucked at the weeds in despair.

CHAPTER 20

The weekend was over. Beckholt resumed work with relief, like a war settling into its humdrum of air raids and tactical manoeuvres.

Sergeant Sheldon drove his panda car past Taunton's cottage on the hour, passing a hundred yards along the lane and walking back each time to speak a word with anyone there, old Stan Deller, Hilda Winner, children cycling, Pete from the village smithy out walking his dog on the playing fields, anyone at all. Word would spread that Joe Sheldon was always along Taunton's lane these days, and safety might then come to the cottage and its occupant . . . maybe.

The launderette resumed its business, the shops opening to provide small congressionals where the women talked and talked. Outside the grocer's shop when Les Taunton walked past a woman cried after her little daughter, "Jane! Jane! Come back in here this minute!" and rushed out to gather the wandering child. Nobody else in there said anything about the traffic, but all the women agreed that you couldn't be too careful. Prams were taken into the small shops creating havoc. One or two bravely asserted they weren't actually nervous, but what with the man of the house working the fields beyond Saints Brook now the baling had started a woman felt alone. After all, they agreed, some of the cottages in Beckholt were so isolated you could see nobody all day long unless you made a special effort to get out. Look what had happened to that girl, Olive. She'd only been going home, hadn't she? And in a place like Beckholt, so much nearer town than some of the other villages. You couldn't be too careful . . .

Reverend Shaw Watson waited after doing his housework and cleaning the kitchen. Mrs. Oldridge usually called before now, wanting the key to the church. Monday was her cleaning day, Thursday her polishing day. After a theft of the silver communion plate the week he'd arrived he'd had to start locking the church, though he bitterly resented having to do so. The parish council, though, had insisted and he'd gone along with them. Finally by eleven he took his own cloths and brushes and crossed into the church to do it himself.

Morning service had been attended by three people, the smallest congregation ever. Communion had enticed two only, and the children's service got a bare dozen. The whole Sunday had sounded hollow, felt quite bizarre. The only bright spot had been Mrs. James, graceful and slim, who had promised to try to help finding a part-time job for Les Taunton though with no great hope of success. For some reason he tried to find words to prolong the brief conversations in the church porch, but as usual his wretched hesitancy condemned him to mere greetings.

Rain started about four in the afternoon, drizzling sombrely with no wind to stir the trees. A chill settled on the day, and night came early. Sunday evensong had started with the church empty. Miss Black, the bespectacled organist, had been missing for the first time in his experience. Hopefully he had delayed the start, searching for reasons to check the vestments again, then he stepped out to the altar and knelt in silent prayer before following the form of evensong in mute solitude. It was only towards the end of the silent service that he realized he was not quite alone. Ashamed by the second presence he avoided looking down the church to see who had entered to kneel in isolation by the church door.

The person had gone by the time he emerged from the vestry after his lonely service. He saw to the candles, replaced the snuffer against the corner, switched off the lights, and locked up. Then out into the drizzle, home. He was almost certain it had been Taunton. The quiet deliberate sounds had been those of a man, he thought.

He read in the rectory that night, seeing the Sunday out in

his study and risking a sherry—risk because it would not do for a late caller to detect alcohol on the priest's breath.

And nobody again to the Monday morning service. And now no cleaner to clean the church. New flowers had appeared on Saturday but they needed some attention, so as to seem at least cared for.

He waited for a minute, letting his eyes accustom to the gloom of the church and hoping Mrs. Oldridge would come. Better not put on the lights, to save money. And the heating could well stay off until late October if the weather continued mild. He wondered idly if it was worth a prayer, requesting the Lord to prolong this weak-kneed summer, but decided that would be the height of presumption. He worried where the best place was to start, finally settled for the altar and promising himself to work towards the west door.

And on the same Monday Taunton was sweeping the forecourt of Terry's garage when Terry drove in. He stared a moment, slammed his car door.

"What the hell are you doing, Taunton?"

"Hello, Terry." Les had been sweeping and tidying for half an hour before Terry had arrived.

"Put that down."

"I come back, Terry—"

"You've not. You've a bloody nerve." Terry looked around. "What do you think's been going on here, while you were away doing bugger all, eh?" Terry thumbed towards the road. "That lot comes here rain or frigging shine, mate. They can't wait for bloody months while you get yourself in and out of scrapes. They're a very fickle mob, them customers. They want service— they want it *now*."

"Is there any chance of doing part-time, like?"

"How the hell do you think I've managed? On my tod? Not likely, mate. I've got a bloke from Colnebridge. I can't give him the chuck just because you've decided to come strolling in like Lord Muck now your jaunt's ended."

Les ran his hand through his hair helplessly. "But I thought—"

"Think somewhere else, mate." Terry took out his keys to unlock the garage office. "I'm a business, not a frigging charity."

A car pulled on to the hard shoulder and started reversing into the garage service area.

"That's my man now. Clear off."

"If anything comes up, Terry," Les said, "like you need an extra hand for a day or two . . ."

Terry rattled the glass in the door and was already examining the morning post.

"Want something, mate?" the man called from the service area. He was in oil-stained overalls.

"No, thanks."

That afternoon Clare wangled herself free for two hours, promising Andy Greig to repay him the earth in surgeries the following week. She let Jackie know and drove into town. "Just shopping," she'd informed her, but parked in the main square and went straight to the reference library. They only had one small newspaper section, but surely they would have the *County Banner* for the period covering Olive Hanwell's murder. She avoided a former patient who saw her and was eager for a chat. She hadn't much time.

CHAPTER 21

"Is this an official call, Inspector?"

"Yes, Doctor. Sorry if it interferes."

"You're very welcome."

Clare's cool voice and official manner were for the receptionist's benefit. Ken had phoned the previous day. It was Sheldon's idea to postpone seeing the priest, and suss out the doctor first. And then maybe to tackle the schoolteacher Edgeworth with better information. Clare had suggested the interval between the surgeries when she could juggle her house calls and with luck spare an hour.

Jackie was replacing the last of the day's records when the inspector came through. Clare pleased her by letting her go earlier than usual, and led Ken into her consulting-room. He was curious, seeing an aspect he had only known at second-hand. They talked desultorily, both listening automatically for the receptionist's departure. When the door finally shut Clare raised a hand to keep him in his chair.

"Stingy."

Clare smiled. "Not here, Ken. Walls have ears—and eyes as well, I shouldn't wonder."

"It's odd." He looked about quizzically. "Of course I've always known you *are* a doctor. But actually seeing the tools of your trade, all this . . ."

"Going to chuck me up?"

"Don't joke, love. I wonder how you can, well, make love, find pleasure in a man's body. You must be sick of anatomy."

"Loving's not anatomy. That's silly. The same would go for a male doctor."

"I suppose so. All the same . . ."

"Doctors would die out, never reproduce." She smiled outright.

"All right, then. In your professional capacity." He waited to give her time. "This guerrilla war in Beckholt."

"It's no such thing, Ken. A few layabouts—"

"It's a war by my definition, Clare," he interrupted bluntly. "And that's what matters. It must stop."

"I heard about the man's cat. Sickening. Sick people."

"It's just war, love. Beckholt versus Taunton."

"That's a contradiction, Ken. Taunton *is* Beckholt, at least in part."

"Not any more. He's extruded. I've seen it happen before. He's outside the pale, and like a fool, trying to pretend otherwise."

"What do you want, Ken?" Her voice was quiet. Events were moving skewed, the correct motion lost. The thought came to depress her that maybe she'd badly misjudged the situation and would have to start again.

"Help, love. Tell me everything you know."

"You know about confidentiality, Ken. I can't simply hand over medical records. But there's nothing relevant in them. I've racked my brains. I've even been to see John Chesterton."

"All right. I accept that, love. This schoolteacher. Edgeworth."

"Ed? He's balanced, extrovert. Fitted in here marvellously by all accounts. The children like him."

"A good opinion?"

"Yes, I'd say so."

"The priest says Edgeworth's worried the village might get savage."

"*Get . . . ?* Doesn't he call what happened to that poor animal 'savage,' for heaven's sake?"

"Savage to Taunton."

"They're already savage to Taunton."

"Word is they might kill him, Clare."

She was appalled at his frankness and sat stricken. "Is it possible?" John Chesterton had said so.

"It was more than that for Olive Hanwell."

"Is it preventable?"

"The funny thing about murder is that we know more or less how many actually happen. An underestimate, but we're not too far out. The converse is unknowable: we simply have no idea how many murders *never* actually have happened—those that could just as easily come about, but for some reason get deflected at the last minute. The intended victim goes blithely on his way unscathed, ignorant of having missed being murdered by a quirk. No way of counting those."

"Which will this be?" She looked tired and worn.

"I want to find out, Clare. Anything you can tell me will help. What people say, how they sound when saying it. Anything."

"You're speaking of intangibles. I'm trained in other things."

"Think of it as mass psychiatry, love."

The headache which had been with her all day worsened. She agreed, feeling exhausted. And this evening promised to be quite a long surgery. Maybe she should accept Andy Greig's offer of a partnership, and take on an assistant doctor, one they could train.

"I'll try, Ken."

"That's why I'll have to see the priest."

"What use will he be?"

"Maybe none."

"To offer a prayer for Taunton's safety?" she snapped with derision. "Taunton needs a police guard, not an invocation to the gods."

"He's got one." Ken eyed her reaction. "And the other, too, for all I know. In any case it was the priest who reported Edgeworth's fears. A brave act. Edgeworth wouldn't tell Sheldon himself. That would have meant naming which children had voiced their parents' feelings. Secrets of the home and all that."

"Brave? *Him?*"

"Mmmm. We counted your allies, love, remember? With Edgeworth disaffected, it's you and the priest. Alone. Is Reverend Watson popular?"

"With my district nurse," Clare said coolly. "Not many others."

"Big congregation?"

"A few hanging on to outmoded superstitions. Oldies. A barmy old organist who tipples in secret and can hardly see the keys. Your average church."

"Don't knock it, love. It might matter."

"In paradise, presumably?"

"You're very down on this bloke, love."

"I'm talking of them all. It's high time they went, Ken. The whole pack of them. Spongers peddling unfounded hopes."

"But him in particular?" he pressed.

She looked away. "He's the most pathetic of them all. Why he doesn't do a proper job like a man . . ."

"What does he think of Taunton's chances?"

"I haven't asked."

Ken waited for her to continue, but she avoided his gaze and said nothing. "Who's the nurse?" he asked at length.

"Esther Batsford. She's not bad, as district nurses go. Conscientious."

"And she's particularly friendly with this priest?"

"I didn't say that." Clare pressed her fingers against her temples, closing her eyes for a moment. "Look, Ken. If that's all, I'd better try to lie down for a few minutes. I've a surgery to do. I'll listen out for you as you asked.

He stopped himself from making a jokey remark and wisely took his leave. Outside in his car he thought a moment before driving to the rectory. Had there been some argument between herself and the priest which she had failed to mention, or was there something more? And this Nurse Batsford was losing favour, that was plain. But maybe gaining favour in another direction entirely?

Clare slipped her shoes off and slumped on the bed. She hadn't experienced one of these heads for months but now her forehead was throbbing and it hurt her eyes to lift her lids. The aspirin would be a few minutes in the working.

Extraordinary how this Taunton business had come about. Quite like an abscess at first, beginning as something rather diffuse then concentrating in a fearsome mound of diseased cells. And now everything seemed to have centred on a few people. Taunton, of course. Ed, that likeable and popular teacher. Not herself, she thought firmly. She was outside it all, in a way made immune by the nature of her work. And of course Sarah Horn and her coven. One couldn't forget them. And last, but it was beginning to seem positively not least, Reverend Shaw Watson, harbinger of religion in a world that had no time for his kind any more . . . But was that true? Ken had doubts.

She turned over irritably. The tablets weren't working as they ought. One more? She decided not to. A clear head for the evening surgery, especially with four antenatals on the list.

Who still said prayers, the way she'd been taught as a little girl kneeling by the bedside? Practically no one. And who for heaven's sake formed a modern congregation, except the elderly with too much time on their hands, possibly subliminally apprehensive of their looming fate? Add to that a few children sent to Sunday school in order to rid the house of them while their parents retired for the afternoon . . .

She pushed herself up on an elbow and thumped the pillow into shape, flopped down again. Yet Ken thought it worth his while to come out himself, to interview the priest instead of leaving it to his subordinates, as she guessed was normal practise. Was it some lingering impulse to consult the local oracle, perform obeisance to the wizard of the tribe? Or was it Ken's policeman's instincts?

But John Chesterton said there'd been nothing in Taunton's medical history to help her in trying to . . . What? Clear him? And why should she bother with criminal matters, with enough medical problems on her plate? One thing was certain, she told herself angrily. Her concern was not to help that . . . that witch doctor. I'll bet the bloody man doesn't even believe in himself, she criticized spitefully. It's all a front. There are men in space every day of the week, footprints on half the planets. This world had simply to decide whether it was going to stay entombed in the Dark Ages, or not. Simple as that.

Children who had suffered covert rheumatic fever were often punished in school for excessive fidgeting when in fact they were often unable to sit still. But John Chesterton knew nothing in Taunton's medical history. Nothing in the medical records that might help. But in Olive Hanwell's . . . ? Head throbbing, she rose and went through to take a quick look at the files before surgery, thinking why she shouldn't leave it till later heaven alone knows . . . She caught at the phrase and told herself that it was only a figure of speech.

"Should you be in here?" Dusty Lang asked, nudging old Deller at the bar.

"One pint does no harm."

"That's what you say," Ned smiled. "I'll tell Doc."

"She'll salt your tail." Dusty guffawed.

"She lets me," old Stan lied. He ordered a pint. Jenny looked doubtfully at the old man but served him anyway.

"Don't go blaming me, Mr. Deller," she warned. "You lot are witnesses. He said he's allowed."

"Mind you, I wouldn't mind putting a bit o'me own salt on Doc's tail." Dusty guffawed again. "She'm a cracker."

"She's a bad temper wi' me lately." The old diabetic drank and felt the beer cold in his belly. He closed his eyes in ecstasy.

"What you been up to, you old devil?"

"Nothing. Good as gold. That nurse is the same."

"I wouldn't mind her, an' all," Dusty said.

"Same here." Ned's persistent smile grew reflectively. "Lovely bike action!"

There was a general laugh. The taproom had not yet filled for the evening and conversation was clearly audible without the juke-box.

"How d'you manage to get on the wrong side o' both on 'em together, Stan?"

"Don't know, Ned. The only time they ever do agree, seems to me."

"What you been tryin' on, you randy old codger?"

"No good with that nurse," Stan replied slyly. "Haven't you young lads heard? Word is she's sweet on the Reverend."

"That right?" Dusty gave Ned a sharp glance. "How long, Stan?"

"Why ask me?" the old man disclaimed all responsibility. "I didn't start this, did I, Jenny? I come in here for a quiet drink."

"Fancy that now," Dusty breathed. "Our vicar and the nurse, eh?"

"I call that real romantic, like." Ned beamed on the crowd. "Happen there'll be a weddin' soon, eh? Wonder who marries a priest? Do 'e do it hisself?"

"Mebbe that Inspector Young's goin' to be the best man," Stan suggested.

"From Colnebridge?" Dusty asked into the short silence.

"Why him, Stan?" Ned beamed.

"He's spending time wi' the Reverend these days."

"Is he, now!" Dusty breathed. He raised his head to where Bob and Frank were talking by the dartboard. Both were looking his way.

"Proper little chatterboxes, these Old Bills." Ned smiled across at Dusty and nodded. "Chatter, chatter, chatter!"

"Wonder why," Dusty prompted, but old Stan was not having any and shook his head.

"Don't ask me."

"Wonder what they got to talk about," Dusty said to Ned carefully.

Ned's enduring smile never faltered. "Oh, this and that," he said. "You know what they're like, Dusty."

"Where's Mick Robie?" Stan asked casually of Jenny. "Thought I'd see him in by now."

"Up at the social club, most like."

"How's all your neighbours, Stan?" Ned enquired innocently. "Hilda Winner, Les Taunton, that lot down your lane?"

"Settling in fine, it looks like. O'course, Hilda's been a great help to Les." He took a good draught of the pint.

"Has she?" Ned smiled benevolently.

"Don't know what he'd have done without her," Stan said evenly.

"After the other night, too, when he scared her nigh to death?"

"Funny things, women."

"Not half as funny as men," Jenny shot in.

"I'd get you another pint, Stan," Ned smiled, inspecting the old man's glass. "But I'm worrit about your health. You know how it is."

"Don't let that stop you, Ned."

"No." Ned put his hand on his heart. "I'd best not. You'd do the same for me, I'm sure."

Laughing, Ned and Dusty went across to join Bob and Frank at the dartboard.

That evening Shaw rang Fogg Powell, Sergeant Sheldon, and the Henriques in their splendid isolation at Ford Farm, all within an hour, to no avail. None had a job they could throw open to Taunton. He tried Terry after that, but one always felt with Terry that you had to start from some bargaining position, and Shaw was made to feel that he had no bargaining counter to begin with.

"I don't get paid for nothing, Reverend," Terry told him politely. "And I don't expect to pay somebody for staying away for months on end, either."

Shaw found he was saying goodbye to a burring receiver.

He tried the village's three shops and was told sorry, there wasn't an opening, and anyway the village girls were preferred who could gain some popularity among the villagers. Shaw said thank you to them all.

He had left Mrs. Davidson until last. The best wine? She was in, amused at the quavering in his voice.

"This is Shaw Watson, Mrs. Davidson. I hope I haven't interrupted—er—I hope I'm ringing at a convenient, er . . ."

She sounded more amused than ever, as if hugging some secret joke to herself that was too good to share.

"I simply can't get used to hearing priests announce themselves *quite* so chattily, Reverend," she observed with pleasant asperity. "As if you were some kind of social worker that has to *project* an *image*. I shall call you Reverend until we're much better acquainted."

"Er, thank you," he said lamely. What was so amusing? A terrible gaffe, interrupting something intimate . . . ? "Er, Mrs. Davidson? I was wondering, erm . . ."

"I'll send twenty pounds, Reverend, but must warn you that—"

"Erm, no." He was sure that she was enjoying herself. "No, thank you. I don't need the money."

"You don't? What sort of a priest *are* you, Reverend? We've never had free religion before, I do assure you!"

"Er, well I do, actually. What I mean was something more important—"

"Good grief," she exclaimed. "Is there no stopping you? Something more important to a priest than money?"

"About Taunton."

"Oh." She sounded sincerely disappointed. "*You* want me to bar Taunton too?"

"Bar him?" Shaw wondered what she had heard. "No. It's about a job for him."

"Go on, Reverend. I'm enjoying this."

"I know you used to give him the occasional task, Mrs. Davidson. Might I ask if you paid him, er . . . ?"

"No, Reverend. I shackled him to an underground wheel. I'm a white slaver."

"You're joking," he said eventually into her laughter.

"Of *course* I paid the man! Why?"

"Could you see your way clear to, erm, well, if you had room, and always providing it caused no hardship to anyone else, erm . . ."

"Give him a job, you mean?"

"Well, yes, please. If, that is . . ."

"Certainly. In fact, I think I've got one waiting. My foreman needs a marshman."

"So he can come? Does Taunton know?"

"No. I believe not. He can just turn up, preferably at some ungodly hour, or my foreman will sulk and we don't want that, do we?"

"Er, quite," he said uncertainly. "Shall I tell him?"

"Pass the word, Reverend, if you would."

"Thank you very much, Mrs. Davidson." The temptation came to risk a small blessing, he decided in a frantic pause that it would sound utterly ridiculous, and thanked her profusely again.

"Not at all," she said. "Oh, one thing."

"Yes?"

"Can you come to supper, Saturday?"

"Me? *This* Saturday?"

"Busy night, I suppose," the lady guessed mischievously.

He blustered, "No, er, no. I don't go out much, er, Mrs. Davidson."

"Seven-thirty," she concluded briskly. "Come fairly unkempt, if you can. And get all your smoking over and done with before you set foot in my place or I'll have a fit."

"Er, thank you, Mrs. Davidson," he said. "I don't smoke, actually."

"It'll be rather boozy, actually," she said. "So gird up your loins."

"Er . . ." He dithered, not knowing whether to say yes he would or change the subject. She said good evening and rang off. He could have sworn she was laughing to herself as she put the receiver down.

He stared at the study wall, wondering what a strange mixture of attributes women seem to possess. Gradually he started smiling. Taunton had a job. A job, the sole means of Taunton's return to normality, to assimilation in the village. He'd done it. Somehow he'd done it.

CHAPTER 22

Shaw found the schoolteacher out on his allotment digging for an autumn sowing. At least Ed was a countryman, if not a local, so he would know the mystique of cabbages and turnips and what crops followed what. To the priest it was all a long unrolling mystery, without laws that could be understood by any townie.

"Hello, Ed."

The teacher straightened up and stared at him with hostility. "Thought better of it, have you?"

"Thought . . . ?" For a moment Shaw did not understand. "Oh. Our misunderstanding."

"No misunderstanding," Edgeworth said. He kicked loose soil from his fork. "Not on my part."

"Well, I came to say all will probably be all right from now on."

Edgeworth's forehead cleared. "That's a relief," he said. "I'm glad you saw sense. Look. I know I rather led off at you, but you must admit it was called for."

"I'm not sure I follow."

"You decided not to phone Sheldon, right?"

"Well, no. I actually *did* contact Sergeant Sheldon—"

"You what? You bloody fool!"

"But let me explain, Ed. It didn't stop there. It's quite resolved."

"You actually contacted Sheldon? And told the police what I said?"

"Yes. But you see that I had to."

"You bloody fool. I ought to knock your head off, you silly sod."

"No. I haven't finished."

"You did something else? Jesus!"

"I've found Les Taunton a job," Shaw inserted quickly. "So it will be fine."

"I don't understand you, you stupid burke." The teacher was shaking his head wonderingly. "You've got him a job? Here? In Beckholt?"

"Yes." Shaw searched Ed's expression, puzzled. "Marshman, down at Mrs. Davidson's farm over at Saints Brook—"

"Then God help Taunton. And God help you, you bonehead. At least I managed to stop Monica James having him help with the school caretaking."

So that explained why that had fallen through. "But I thought you'd be glad it's all over."

"Get on your bike, priest." Ed waved him away. "You're just not real. You're stupid as well as blind. Piss off, man."

"But what's wrong?" The priest was bewildered. "Can't you see? They'll take him back, stop treating him like an incomer." His plea became passionate, wanting reassurance and approval. "They'll begin talking to him, stop these dangerous cruelties. Within a week it'll be plain sailing. You'll see. It's just a question of contact between them and Taunton."

The teacher cut at him, "I'll tell you what'll happen, Reverend. Within a week you'll be gone from here. The village will have spit you out like a fucking pip. And your precious lunatic Taunton will be dead. Dead as Olive Hanwell. I may be an incomer, like you, *Reverend*." He spat the title from him with distaste. "But there's one slight difference. I go with them, because they're the society here. In other words I'm an incomer with sense. You're an incomer who stays ignorant, who never learns. You poor fucking idiot. Get gone."

"You can't be right, Ed."

"Reverend," Edgeworth said wearily, almost pleadingly. "Reverend, please. There's a good bloke. Just piss off and take the consequences."

The priest had gone a few paces only when the teacher called after him.

"And Reverend."

"Yes?" Shaw paused hopefully.

"Don't come to me for help, whatever you do. You'll get none."

Shaw left, walking unsteadily on the grassway between the allotments. There was some local skill in walking unmuddied along these raised grassy cuts between dug ground but of course it was a local art and he knew nothing of it. He was wet round his ankles with mud by the time he reached the road.

Les reported to Bertie on time, and was immediately sent to get a folder from the Hall farmhouse, a clear ruse on Bertie's part to speak with the five men. He ledged himself on a cart to speak, his horse Shakespeare, a tall English hunter too disdainful for anything but riding a manager's rounds, waiting impatiently nearby.

"You fellers'll be wonderin'," he said to them, his breath fogging the air round the yard as he spoke. "Well, I'll stop that in short order."

"He comin' to work again here, Bertie?" asked Dando, a sour tractorman who had worked all his life at the Hall Farm.

"Yes, Dando."

"Is he allowed?" That for a small toothy man known as Sparrow, one of the few Fieldham men to work this side of the Saints Brook. "I heard tell he'll be barred the village."

"That's to be seen, Sparrer. But I got somethin' to say to youse." He spat expertly into a pool a few yards off. This man's comin' here again. He'll be our marshman. Reeds are cloggin' the Saints Brook as far as the ruins near the far copse, and the farm needs them cleared—and for sellin'. Now you might not like that. I might not like it. And sure as hell the village ain't goin' to like it. You'll all have heard that. Right?"

"Right, Bertie."

"Now, what the village wants is one thing. But what Mrs. Davidson and Hall Farm wants is a different thing entirely. There's no call to make differences where there is none. But a stand's a stand. And Mrs. Davidson's promised Taunton a place."

"He were part-time," Joe Robie said. Joe was nothing like the size of his cousin Mick but for all that represented a formidable part of the manpower at Hall Farm. He was thick-chested, known to wrestle well and was notable in the tug-o'-war competition which the village pubs organized every Easter.

"So he were," Bertie gave back. "But he's full-time now."

"That don't seem right."

"What's wrong wi' it, Joe?"

"There's other lads in the village'd be glad of a job, especially marshman."

"I heard." Bertie's gaze did not waver.

"It should go to a decent Beckholt man, Bertie, not a murderer. That's all I'm sayin'."

There came a murmur of agreement from the four Beckholt men. Sparrow wisely remained silent. He merely resolved to keep a wary eye on Taunton, especially while he was wielding that billhook, and kept his own counsel.

"He'm as much a Beckholt man as you, Joe," Bertie said mildly.

"I say he has no place here," Joe Robie growled, emboldened by Bertie's apparent hesitancy.

"Balls, Joe Robie."

"Eh?"

"You heard, Joe." Bertie stood upright. "Now listen to me. This man Taunton's coming here. Today. He starts as marshman. Who he is doesn't matter a toss to me. D'you hear? Not a tinker's fuck. The farm's everything. Everything. It's your wages and your bread. It's tomorrow's reason for gettin' out uv your pits. It's the reason the cows get milked and slaughtered in season. It's the reason we keep goin', and happen if enough of us sees sense like that, well then, there'll be a few farms survive i' the country to see next year out, no matter what bloody daftness spins round in your heads."

He stared evenly at them into stillness.

"Now, I've said my say. Anybody disagree?"

There was a taut silence. Joe Robie looked about to speak but Bertie slowly stepped forward a pace. He was a dangerous man in a fight, as at least three of them could testify from bitter experience.

"What about you, Joe Robie?" Bertie rasped. "That Mick of yourn's had a deal to say and do by all accounts."

"So what?" Joe muttered, gauging the reactions of the other workers.

"So I'm askin' you outright if you're going to take a swing." Bertie moved closer. "If you've a mind, let's get started, then I'll just break a couple of your chestbones and we can all get down to farmin' and have done wi' this woman's talk."

Dando laughed at the calm foreman. Sparrow too grinned at hearing the morbid Dando cackling so unexpectedly.

"I'll not fight over such as he," Joe Robie said sulkily.

"Any time you change your mind, Joe," Bertie offered, "you just go runnin' to your Mick and tell 'e as well. I'll perish the both of 'e. You follow?" Bertie tapped Joe's thick chest, shoving him a pace backwards. "I said, d'you follow?"

"Yes," Joe Robie said, his eyes murderous.

"Mind you do, lad," Bertie said quietly. "Either o'you come at me and I'll see the both of you off. Now." He wagged an arm. "Get farmin'," the idle lot o' you."

Les Taunton was sent to reed the stream. On the Essex border, the reeds were thinner and not so tall as in the northern parts of

East Anglia. With the narrowness of the rivers, too, there was less chance of using a proper reed punt as they did in the fens. The custom had built up in past ages of using a horse-drawn cart, blue-painted and high on the axles, for carrying the reeds by the sides of the smaller streams of the region, with the marshman cutting by wading or from steps on the cart's sides.

Les Taunton had done the job before and walked the horse down to Saints Brook to start the cutting. Reeds were always a valuable property, but he knew the reed crops had increased as the importance of thatching had finally been realized, and since marginal crops were now proving vital elements in the survival of many farms.

He was a careful worker, leaving fewer wasted stems and less untidiness than any of the other five labourers, so Bertie had given him the stretch from the valley point, where the village's Colnebridge road crossed, down to the old church ruins in the copse. There was sometimes a certain amount of illicit hunting and poaching that way over but Bertie never minded that. Kept down some of the fallow deer and other predators which proved so destructive to many of the crops.

Les left the horse and cart downstream and came towards the copse, walking the narrow river before starting. Any unexpected fallen branches in the water tended to mean a lack of crispness in the reeds along the length of the damned-back stretch. There were local sayings advising against cutting of reeds near stagnant water. Walking the stretch only took a few minutes and showed to his satisfaction that the stream was clear. All its debris had been carried down in the recent heavy rains, a boon when he wanted to start work immediately and show how right Bertie and Mrs. Davidson had been to trust him.

He saw something move in the thickets down near the old ruins and went to a small tumulus to scan the undergrowth from above. The ruins showed clearly. A fallow deer was grazing there, its ears on the go as always and stopping to scent round itself. Not often you got such a sighting. There were some folk as couldn't see such without wanting to shoot it down, all for nothing. He gazed at the ruins. They showed through the grass here and there. Having played so often as a kid among them, he knew where to look for the greyish stones, but a stranger might take it for a simple clearing in the thicket. I dare say, he chuckled to himself, the town museum'll be scratching over there with them students in a hundred years' time. They could do their digging now and save all that bother. The ruins stuck up clear as day if you knew where to look!

It had been a warm day, that time he and Olive Hanwell had walked down there, with her telling how she and Bertie'd got together and loved. She'd been a shocker, poor old Olive had, telling such things. Out with it, right plain as all day, as if it was a joke or somethin' to talk of what a man did to a woman, and how a woman acted to get him going. Ar, and what things a woman did to a man an' all. She'd even imitated Bertie's groans and cries, then lifted her skirt to show the marks of Bertie's nails and the deep bruising where his body and hands had flailed upon hers.

"We did it three times," she'd told Les that day long ago down in the church ruins along the Saints Brook. "How old Joany in that great Hall of hers keeps up with him I'll never know. Like a bull he was. Didn't talk much, though, and I like a man to talk to me a bit, say nice things and show appreciation. But I'm not complainin'—Bertie's good. Heavy as an old shire!"

Les had reprimanded her for talking so, but that only set her off laughing more. She'd glanced at him mischievously at that and asked what kind of things he liked doing. She pulled his leg, jokingly accusing him of going with various village girls and shrieking astonishment when he finally admitted he'd never had a girl himself.

In the ruins she had taken him in her hands, gently and with great care bringing him to orgasm, cooing and gentling him to love which astonished him. The sensation was beyond belief. It was uncontrollable, electrifying. She'd carried one of those pocket radios which had played distorted music as they had loved in the tall grass of the clearing. Amazingly, she had not been offended as he penetrated her. Even more astonishing had been her acceptance of his weight and the discomfort which must surely have resulted from his body lying on hers.

She had been shaking him, though, worried, some time afterwards when he came to. "God!" she'd exclaimed as he'd woken. "I was giving you up for dead! You went right off. If I'd known shaggin' did that to you, Les Taunton, I'd ha' thought twice about it, straight I would!"

A hand clouted him out of his reverie. He staggered and all but fell forward. The foreman was standing there, Shakespeare tethered to a gorse bush a hundred yards off.

"I tellt you to get on, Taunton," Bertie snapped. "Not stand gapin' at the trees. Get on. You've been an hour and done sod all. That's an hour's extra time you'll put in this day. D'you hear?"

"I'm sorry, Bertie," Les stammered, confused. An hour? It could only have been a minute at most. He started back downstream at a clumsy run to where the horse and cart waited. "I'll do well, you'll see!"

"Dozy sod," Bertie muttered. He paused to stare down at the ruins, wondering what could have intrigued the stupid man for such a long spell, saw nothing and shook his head. Having given the man a job and gone to the line for him, he'd make sure the blighter worked, murder or no murder.

CHAPTER 23

Sarah Horn faced George Falconer, her basket clasped in front of her.

"A word, George."

"Any time for you, Mrs. Horn."

"You can stop that. I'm not one of your motor-cars full of

passing strangers who'll take anything you have to offer as long as you give good cheer with it. I've come to say we're losing, George."

"Losing?"

"You know well what I mean. The fight to rid our village of that murderer. Taunton's got a job on that harlot's farm, for reasons we dare not think about. And that kept man of hers has sided with her, as is only natural seeing as he knows which side his bread's buttered. Bertie's not the first to have sold his soul for a mess of pottage."

"How can we prevent that, Mrs. Horn?"

They stopped the conversation by mutual consent while he served carrots and runner beans to a family in a Mini. Sarah Horn gazed stonily across the road, ignoring the car lady's friendly remarks about the weather prospects. The car pulled away.

"By causing him to leave, George Falconer. You well know how it's done. It's been done before, when incomers have proved troublesome."

A few days earlier George would have protested, albeit mildly enough, about Les Taunton's incomer status but now he accepted the designation without comment.

"I'm uncertain what the rest think, Mrs. Horn."

"You're not, George." Her voice lowered for the confidence. "Nobody else is. You just want to sit on the fence till the village declares itself. Trust your judgement, George Falconer—like the rest. Trust it! Stand firm! I've spoken to Nathaniel and Zuleika. Teacher Edgeworth is uncorrupted now, the Lord be praised for His great bounty! Eric Carnforth always was sensible. He knows his duty. That priest—that *heathen* priest—has shown his true colours from the moment the killer came in here, so we know who the enemy is."

She spoke as if Taunton was a complete stranger. George said, distressed, "I'll think about it, Sarah."

"There's too little time, George Falconer. The arrows are in the air, shot either for or against evil."

"He's got the law's protection."

Sarah said without relenting, "We have a special right over this man."

"Not above the law, Sarah."

"*Yes* above the law! To one side of the law, if it pains you so much! We have the right to decide our own verdict—never mind what those legal fools said! This man was once one of *us*, part of the village. Like an infant was once part of its parents."

"That's stretching things, Sarah," George said unhappily, pulled into her ferocious argument under the influence of her bright hypnotic stare.

"Is it, George Falconer? Has a mother, a father, no rights over their child, then? Or do they have some say over and above the law?"

"Well . . ."

"You know the rights of it. A parent has responsibilities, George Falconer. To the child. What must be done must be done."

"But who's to do . . . ?"

"The parents, George Falconer. The parents. Us."

"Have you spoken to Eric?" George wished fervently that a horde of travellers would happen by, get him away from this decision.

"Teacher Edgeworth and Nathaniel Jones are with him now. Edgeworth was more disturbed than any of us but his heart was always right. You could tell at a glance."

"I can't think for the minute, Sarah."

She hissed, "Courage, George Falconer. You're the leader of the village council. People listen to you. They'll be delighted—and they'll be against you if you're not. No villager ever sided with the incomers and dared stay. You know that—you've said it often enough in the past."

"I'll see Eric and the others."

"Good man. Go in praise of the Lord, George Falconer." She laid a hand on his arm in astonishing familiarity, her cheeks red with zeal. "No duty is easy. Remember that. Duty done is often a saddening thing. God bless, George."

"God bless, Sarah."

Ignoring a slowing car full of smiling occupants, he drew down the sun blind of his stall and hurried inside to speak with Mary.

Clare did not let Mrs. James know she would call, just dropped by on the off-chance. Monica James was gardening, meticulous with a Sussex basket and gloves.

The headmistress was only in her early thirties, small and pretty as a dancer. Clare felt a slight envy. She was one of those women who would look small and pretty to her dying day. She seemed pleasantly surprised at receiving an unexpected caller and came down the path to meet her.

"What a relief!" she exclaimed humorously. "A reason to stop weeding!"

Clare felt welcome, and complimented the teacher on the neatness and vigour of her garden.

"I shall see you get some of these dahlias, Doctor, before you go. We'll have tea first."

"Actually, you're very kind, but I came to ask your help."

"About this Taunton man, I suppose?"

"When he was a child."

"In school?" Mrs. James placed her basket on the path and stripped off her gloves. "I'm afraid I can't help, Doctor. The police asked all those questions. The only one of us who'd remember what the boy was like would be Mr. Downs, and he never had him in his class."

Mr. Downs was middle-aged, and the oldest of the few teachers at the little school.

"Not Mrs. Houghton? Or Mrs. Seddon?"

"Not really. Mrs. Houghton's only part-time, you know, and only moved in to this district two years ago. Mrs. Seddon's near to retiring, and only took general music and girls' classes when Les Taunton was with us."

They walked indoors, Monica ushering Clare into the kitchen.

"Did you not hear anything, ever?" Clare persisted. "Some remark, any comment about Taunton, when people were discussing his arrest? Anything."

"Nothing, I'm afraid. Couldn't Dr. Chesterton help?"

"I've tried him. Gives him a clean bill of health."

"Is it his early behaviour you want to know about?" Monica had the kettle going and was seeing to the cups. "I suppose they went into all that."

Clare said, "The newspaper reports of his trial said nothing about his early days."

Monica became interested. "You've checked on that?"

"I felt I had to."

"Why?"

"Because Taunton doesn't seem the sort of person."

The teacher sighed. "I wouldn't be too sure. Mrs. Seddon said Badger could be a real handful. I know that's no real guide—"

"Badger?"

"It's his nickname, or was at school."

"Why that?"

"Who knows children?" Monica smiled. "Not even Ed would claim to understand them, and look how successful he's been."

"Didn't you say that Mrs. Seddon never taught the boy, though? How would she know if he was a handful?"

"Oh. General music. He was banished from it for good for misbehaving. Some children take to it. Some don't. I wish there was a way of getting them all interested. Music is a great educator, vastly underrated."

"Did he misbehave in other classes?"

"His record says not. The police have photocopies of them all."

During tea Clare asked if Monica James would mind her calling on the elderly Mrs. Seddon. The teacher said of course not, and never asked for enlightenment. Clare decided she liked her a great deal.

Bertie never smoked in Joan's bedroom. On occasional nights he would rise, pad silently out to the adjoining dressing-room and smoke a small cigar there. Before Joan it had been cigarettes. This night when he returned, avoiding switching the light on to prevent her waking, she reached for him and brought her leg across his thighs.

"You've been having one of your filthy smokes, Bertie. I can smell it."

"Reading."

"I'm glad. I was so proud about Dickens." She had persuaded him to read all of those. She pulled him closer across the bed. "You could hardly *spell* at first . . . Quite good at other things, of course."

"What was the idea, asking that priest on Saturday?"

"I'm inquisitive. You know that."

"It's bad ground, Joan."

"Tomorrow I'll phone Dr. Salford, ask her."

"You ill?"

"No, silly. For supper, Saturday."

"Is it a big do? I'm not so keen."

"We haven't had a supper party in *years*, Bertie." She giggled, feeling him rise under her palm. "Too busy."

"We have one every week."

"Only with the Colnebridge crowd. I mean an *extra* one. People from the village."

"Who else'll be coming?"

"I've not decided. But speaking of *coming* . . ."

CHAPTER 24

Clare drove over to the cottage to meet Ken about six o'clock that Wednesday evening. The East Anglian weather was sparkling, the late sunshine warm and brilliant and hedgerows green and lush. Andy Greig was standing in, but Clare would do the Fieldham well-baby clinics Thursday and Friday to repay her sudden request. Andy had been flippant, asking if she was seeing a bloke on the sly and did all this extra time off mean that he had a rival. She drove smiling. There was nothing between them but he had been pleasant and entertaining company on the few occasions they'd met socially.

Ken was pleased she phoned and managed to cut from duty. His car was there when she arrived and she noted with pleasure that he had trimmed some of the grass near the little well.

"*And* I'm painting the window." Ken came out to hold her in welcome.

"I can't smell any paint." She embraced him with relief.

"That's because I haven't started. I'm still at the defilthing stage."

He took her hamper and together they went indoors, arms linked. "Caviare and chips, love?"

"Nothing so elementary. Salmon salad, wholemeal loaves and a cunning chocolate concoction. I've slaved to find time to throw it together. You'll have to brew up."

"Kettle's on. You should hire a serf."

"My only pleasure," she told him, flinging her coat across her armchair, "is shutting people out and deciding my own level of tidiness."

She wandered through the rooms while Ken made the tea. When negotiating for Dr. Chesterton's practise she had looked about, found the cottage and bought it with some vague idea of using it as a retreat on odd days off. But that was before she realized in full the relentless demand of general practise, where she was expected to be on immediate call every one of the hundred and sixty-eight hours in every slogging week—unless, by dint of accepting the onus of another doctor's emergencies she could guarantee an uninterrupted sleep the night following when he repaid the courtesy and did her calls.

But a place was essential, even though the lonely little place wasn't much: two up, two down, and now a loo and shower which she had added, a small straggling garden of trees with lost patios and a well. On a good evening, like now, the estuary's thin line could be seen eight miles off. The air was warm and clear, and white gulls glided easily high over the low country- side. The only other dwellings were two farm cottages two miles away to seaward.

She heard Ken's whistling and the teapot go. Was a secret man essential too? Ken, she thought in a rare moment of ani- mosity towards him, has his secret lover—me. What do I have? I have him, that's what I have. But *do* I actually *have* him? If I have to skulk over to meet him only when I know his children are safely back home from school and the village won't notice and his duty has been arranged and Enid isn't acting up . . . ? Did everybody need a secret lover?

Ken called her in. She went to arrange the food on the low table. The cottage was only sparsely furnished. It had been done in a great hurry when she realized that Ken's transfer was per- manent and their arrangements would work out. So much luck had been involved.

"I've been thinking about you, Ken." She distributed the salad, folding the wrappings away. They settled on the settee. "And partnerships."

He quietened and poured for them both. "I'll need more clues than that, Clare."

"I've been wondering whether to double up with Andy Greig."

"More time off?"

"Certainly. And give the patients a choice."

"Good idea, love. Will the village like it?"

Clare jabbed her fork at the salmon. "Damn the village! I'm sick of worrying whether the village will approve of every bloody thing I do!"

"Don't let them get to you."

"I feel—" she searched irritably for the word—"parasitized, spied on. It's all too inbred, Ken, too bloody fraught. It's unhealthy, somehow."

"Has it always been there, Clare, or is this new?"

She smiled ruefully. "Your bobby's helmet's showing, darling. Oh, I suppose it's been growing. Out there in the garden just now I was thinking of secret lovers."

He pulled her face against his. "What's brought this on, Clare?" He leant off to search her expression.

"Oh, things." She was speaking listlessly. "There's a Mrs. Davidson in the village. Rather a scandal, really. I'm going over to supper on Saturday. She set her cap at one of her farm labourers years ago, 'improved' him as they used to say in Victorian days, education and that. Now he's her foreman, manager, whatever."

"Good for her."

Clare glanced at him. "That's what I think, too, Ken. She got rid of his wife. They say money changed hands, the man's wife was served notice to leave the tied cottage. Stick and carrot. David and Bathsheba but the other way round." She toyed with a piece of lettuce. "Good for her, I say, too."

"You thinking of us, love?"

"I suppose so. It all comes down to having nerve, doesn't it? Or the desire, the lot. I've a notion that the village people only pretend to find her outrageous, and that deep inside everybody admires her. There *is* something rather awe-inspiring in determination, isn't there?"

"I know what you mean." Ken was thoughtful. "Was there a risk?"

"That Bertie would go and simply lose his job but stick to his wife and children? I suppose there was. Doesn't that make it even more breathtaking? A risk taken?"

"A *calculated* risk. Remember she knew him."

"But still a risk. And she won."

Ken said unhappily, "I don't know, Clare, love. It sounds so simple, said like that. In her case maybe it was. It's not always that clear-cut."

"It can't have seemed simple to her, not then. Looked at now, from this distance, of course it appears uncomplicated. We're seeing it from the outside." She put her plate down and sipped her tea. "It'd resolve things, wouldn't it?"

He tried pleasantry. "And end the secret love bit, you mean?"

"Maybe that has a finite life anyway."

"Could we manage without, Clare?" His tactic had failed.

"You just said yourself everybody needed a hidden love for themselves."

"That priest doesn't," she answered lightly.

"Doesn't he?"

"What did you think? You went to the rectory."

"Why are you so interested?"

"I'm not interested *in* him. Of course I'm not. But he seems to be in the thick of this Taunton business. And that's all the village has focused on lately."

"It might blow over."

"Well?" She was waiting.

"Your priest?" he said reflectively. He made a sandwich of his remaining salmon and added tomato slices. "A bright bloke, deep down. Difficult bloke to get to know in one short visit. Not exactly the sort you can invite confidences from, is he?"

"Did you take to him?"

"Yes. I think I did. He's worried sick about doing the right thing."

"Everybody has a conscience, Ken. What's so marvellous about that?"

"Nothing. But his is in daily use. That's pretty unusual. Look at Edgeworth."

"What about Edgeworth?" she asked quickly.

"He's a wise man, at least people'd say so." His tone was ironical. "You can't blame him."

"Did he back down, then?"

"Of course he did. Said Watson had got the wrong idea from some casual remark he'd never made in any case."

"It's a natural response."

"Thoroughly admirable," Ken said drily.

"What sets Watson above us?" she demanded angrily.

"Cool down, love. I don't think he would claim that, would he?"

"He seems bent on keeping the whole rotten business going!"

"That's impossible."

"Well, I'm beginning to think that without that stupid ditherer this problem would vanish!"

"Maybe. But if your priest let the *problem* vanish, Taunton might vanish as well."

Clare flared up. "Don't keep calling him *my* priest!"

"Sorry." He tried to grin. "It's just that whenever we make love these days we finish up talking about him."

She rose and went to the window to look out at the back garden. A small cloud obscured the sun for a moment, making her suddenly reach for her cardigan. The warmth seemed to have gone from the day though it's brightness remained undiminished.

"I'm sorry, Ken," she said over her shoulder.

Shaw worked late in the church. Attendance at choir rehearsal that evening had been abysmal, and finally he had put the best possible face on things and sent them home. All three of them. And the organist had not showed again.

He had fetched flowers from his own garden, seven roses of assorted colours. They'd win no prizes for arranging, but they were something. He cleaned the brasses by taking them over to the rectory and listening to the concert on the BBC, one of his favourites. The Albinoni oboe pieces were so beautiful. It would have been marvellous to have a stereo with maybe a small collection of records.

By evening he'd done his letters and the bookwork. Accounts, bills, letters to the diocese and replies to an American from Idaho who wanted to trace an ancestor. It all needed attention. Then the choice—was it a choice in this day of biochemical determinants of emotion and will? The choice was to listen to the evening discussion programme or to finish cleaning the church. Dark in an hour, so why not leave it until tomorrow? Mrs. Oldridge might have decided to come in by then. But the alternative was: dark in an hour, so why not use that mere hour to finish cleaning the church? A Roman would of course issue a stern reprimand to the laity and let them sink into the eternal flame for backsliding. He smiled at his rueful criticism, probably quite unjustified, and set off to do the church.

He worked well, carrying the filled bucket round to the heap of compost behind the church and being careful with the petals and the dust. Of course he'd forgotten newspapers, and in any case the Sunday paper—his one extravagance—had to be used for leavings and his kitchen peelings at the rectory. The dustpan was an ancient metal thing and the plastic brush was falling to bits. The rectory broom wasn't too decrepit, though. Polish was the main expense. It never seemed to go as far as polish used to. Maybe he spread it wrongly.

He ran out of polish about halfway down the pews. In the gathering dusk he was not able to see very well, having left the lights off for economy. The pews he had done would look no different. He tutted irritably. It all seemed so thankless. And the run of pipes down the middle of the church under the pews were an embarrassment. Thick with dust. Still, sufficient unto the day, he thought. One last tidy of his things and he could leave the quiet church for the night.

He had wasted the day, if you looked at it squarely. Wasted. No choir practise worth mentioning. A sense of mistrust on the faces of the people he'd met. No callers, which was unusual. A growing awareness of the gap between himself and the villagers . . . alienation was the modern term for it. The church helpers not in evidence. The organist and the wardens, the choirmaster. All missing, or in hiding, though one was possibly on holiday— though here too he might at least have let the priest know he'd be away. Or was it a shrewd political move on his part . . . ?

He tidied the cleaning things away, but worried over the empty polish tin. It might come in useful. Wrong to waste, in these days of conservation. But could a polish tin be cleaned? One thing after another. He smiled at his hopeless indecisiveness. Maybe one day the good Lord might see fit to answer his prayers and lend him a little more resolve. Plus, he added mentally, a lesser tendency to embarrassment. A thicker skin. But would that bring even less understanding? Better stay as he was, warts and all.

He hesitated a minute, looking at the altar rail. The external form of prayer had never appealed to him, seeming too pretentious and being open to that most terrifying of all sins, presumption. How hopeless he was, dithering over the simple problem of whether to kneel down while saying a short prayer in his own church. Who else would find a problem in that, for heaven's sake?

He settled it by kneeling, encouraging himself by the fact that he was alone. Nobody would see him praying and think him pretentious since the church door was only a little ajar and the churchyard hedge cut off the view of the church's interior from the road. And it was now frankly almost night. He knelt to pray, his face in his hands. I'm sorry, Lord. I will try to do better. Especially about this Taunton business. My mind must be precise, more certain. The man needs protection. I've seen to it that he has that. The police inspector called Young seemed interested in how the village was behaving towards Taunton, asked how he could help. Seemed aware, too, of the difficulties between the factions here. I gather he had discussed the whole affair with Dr. Salford.

And about her, Lord. Well, all right. I admit it. I'm afraid I've hardly made a great hit there, Lord. My fault, as usual. The old problem of the knowledgeable scientist and the priest. Jam today or jam tomorrow, I suppose, though Nurse Batsford expressed it in rather kinder terms. Anyway, Lord. I harbour a growing *belief* that molecules are hardly the ultimate explanation for anything. And if called upon to do so, he added, fervent for accuracy, I could give reasons for my belief in this matter. To concentrate like she does on science to the exclusion of existence is a load of clag, Lord. It's like slimming by standing on bathroom scales for a month and doing nothing else except watch the scales fall; it can be done, but life's not only that. Life has character. No diamond has only one facet. Okay, I have no medical knowledge or explanations to prove her wrong. I could no more disprove Dr. Clare Salford's management of Betty Woodruff's venereal disease than fly. But I don't *have* to prove or disprove. I can simply alleviate Betty's distress when she comes for solace, and try to defend her as best I can from her mother's blazing fury. She sees it as a punishment. You slung at Betty for her sin with young Vance. Surely I'm entitled to do something else besides stare in awestuck wonder at Dr. Clare Salford's technology?

He paused, wondering if he had gone too far. Sorry, he prayed. I went on a bit there, Lord. Thank You. He rose, dusted off his cassock from kneeling, and turned to go, hesitated. The church was in pitch darkness. The faint shape of the aperture at the far end of the central aisle was gone. He squinted. He could see the shape of the high windows. But the lighter area which should be the space of the half-open doorway was missing. Somebody had put the door to while he had been praying.

He felt a faint wash of unease. Possibly somebody had come in quietly and was praying back there. Or maybe from kindness an unseen hand had pulled—*pushed from inside?*—the big oaken door to. Perhaps only to prevent interruption.

He walked a couple of paces, stopped. His heart was thumping, the banging of it shaking his chest. It must be clearly audible to them. To them? Now why had he thought *them?* Was somebody in the church with him? Singular or plural?

There was no need to get alarmed, nor to show any fear. "Hello?" he said cautiously.

He took another two or three steps, the sound echoing to either side.

"Yes?" he said conversationally. His voice quavered maddeningly.

No answer. There was nothing for it. He walked slowly forward, saying again, "Is anyone there? Are you looking for me?" How silly if nobody was there.

He reached the end of the pews, paused. He heard something outside. A smooth shuffle, the countryman's walk.

"What is it?" he said. Maybe the children were having him on, but it was a stupid game if that was the case. And so late. They'd all be in bed. He was frightened, his heart racing and banging loud enough to wake the dead.

He was a few paces clear to the door. He took them quickly, finding determination from fear, and tugged on the handle. The night air washed mercifully on his face as the door came ajar. He stepped out, smiling at his foolish fears, though his hand was shaking almost uncontrollably as he put the great key in the lock, third go. How silly, he admonished himself as he left the porch and walked between the overhanging trees to the gate.

That sound was obviously one of my parishioners taking a short cut through the churchyard.

He came to the scrollwork iron gate. Odd, that too was closed.

· "Who's there?" he found himself saying. He drew the vertical bolt and the gate squealed gently open. A car's headlights swept the dark from the distant row of high trees. He quickly peered round but the close blackness was absolute as ever under the trees. "Hello?"

His impulse was to drag the gate to and run across the lane to the houses opposite but thought of the ridiculous spectacle that would create, a spooked priest bursting in upon a family somnolently watching telly. He'd disgraced his calling enough without adding ridicule.

He stepped out into the lane. Something scuffed behind him.

"What is it?" he was saying when a blow out of the blackness staggered him. He reeled against the gate, not knowing what was happening.

"What is it?" he said again when they came at him, kicking and clubbing.

"Please don't," he said once before falling against the base of the hedge. They kicked him down then, smashing blows on him from the pitch dark. He heard the scrabbling and shufflings with amazement, utter amazement, and realized the cloutings did not hurt, not physically. It was as if the organism that he was had its own ability to diminish the most painful sudden injuries. The science of it all, he was stupidly thinking. Perhaps this design permitted organisms to respond quickly despite injuries received . . .

CHAPTER 25

"So if we say to start about eightish, you can come about seven to seven-thirty. All right?" Joan Davidson blew Bertie a kiss across the room and beamed into the receiver. "We do look forward to your company, Mrs. James—very well, Monica. Thank you for accepting. 'Bye. 'Bye."

She replaced the receiver and turned the television volume up again as she crossed to where Bertie was dozing on the sofa. She sank beside him.

"Isn't that wonderful? Only the Inspector to go and we're a full complement!"

"What's it for?" He knew Joan.

"This little supper? Let's call it . . . interest, Bertie."

"You can be interested without giving a supper."

"Now, now. Don't be boorish." She closed her eyes and rubbed her head against his thick body. "I want to see them close to. Suddenly, I need to know what this oddness actually is. The village *looks* absolutely normal but *feels* turgid, explosive." She smiled.

"About Taunton, Joan."

She opened her eyes. "What about him? He's not coming, if that's what you mean."

"Did you ever go with him?"

She smiled to herself at the thick jealousy in his voice. "Of course not," she said evenly. "And is that a question to ask of a lady?"

"You asked me about Olive Hanwell."

"That's different. She was never a lady."

Clare drew into the surgery drive as Jackie Hughes came rushing out into the headlights. Clare's first thought was that there had been a break-in, some burglar perhaps . . . The receptionist was almost hysterical with excitement. She wrenched open Clare's driving-side door, shrieking, "Doctor! Doctor! Where've you been?"

Clare was startled and fumbled the handbrake ratchets into place.

"Whatever's the matter, Jackie? Dr. Greig's on call until I got back. I told—"

"He's been ringing! The priest—"

"Priest? Which priest?"

"Reverend Watson! He's been hurt—"

"How badly?" She felt the car jerk forward and shudder to a stall. She'd still been in gear. "How badly?"

"They got him by the church, all blood! The police—"

Clare's heart almost stopped. "What happened?"

"Dr. Greig's there, Doctor, and he wants—"

"*Where*, you stupid woman?"

Clare's stinging rebuke fetched Jackie wide-eyed to her senses. "At the rectory, Doctor."

Clare gunned the engine. "Get my bag. *Hurry*."

"Yes, Doctor." Jackie rushed off and emerged with the huge black bag by the time Clare had the motor turned. Clare snatched it from the receptionist in a savage temper.

"You could have had it with you, instead of running about shrieking," she snapped, letting in the clutch and leaving Jackie in a shower of gravel.

She accelerated down towards the scout hut, swinging wide round Nurse Batsford who was cycling along Church Road towards the rectory. She had the sense to sound her horn briefly as she overtook the hurrying figure. She knew she'd spoken too sharply to Jackie Hughes, but honestly . . .

The rectory gate was obscured by the crowd of villagers who nudged each other as the car was recognized. She slammed the door and pushed through without an apology, thrusting her emergency bag forward, using it as a weapon to push the stupid people out of the way. One or two muttered a greeting but she ignored them and ran past the police constable who raised his hand imperiously to stop her.

The rectory was a blaze of lights. She half-noticed that the church was illuminated by a kind of floodlight worked from a machine, presumably some sort of generator the police had brought. A man in plain clothes impeded her.

"I'm Detective-Sergeant Hawksmoor. Who—"

"Dr. Salford."

Clare rushed past. Andy Greig was seated at the head of the sofa, leaning over the battered figure of the priest and still cleaning the wounds. Bowls and blood, Clare thought dully. This rectory's nothing but bowls and blood.

"Andy?"

The medical man looked up casually, retaining pressure of a dressing pack on an open scalp wound. His eyes were about to return to his task after giving her a cursory greeting but paused, locked on hers for an instant.

"Knocked to blazes. Seven lacerations, apparently by boots, heavy instruments. A lot of damaged tissue. I'm afraid of a fracture. There's a hell of a sogginess over the right temporal."

She knelt beside her colleague, tore open the bag to assist. "Anything else?"

"Cracked ribs, almost certain. Badly bruised. Nothing spinal, limbs okay."

"Conscious?"

"Must have been at some point. Alan from the shop found him, walking that spaniel."

"Does he respond?"

"Stimuli? Nothing internal in his nut, as far as one can tell for the minute."

Clare examined the priest's face. It was swollen and bruised almost beyond recognition. She questioned Andy with a mute glance, received a silent assent and gently palpated the temples and over the frontal region. The orbits were mercifully spared, almost the only part of his face left intact. The skin over the mandibular area was almost scarified. "Not a road accident."

"Not a chance, Clare," Andy muttered angrily. He was done over."

"Abdominal?" She pulled away the blanket covering the priest's frame.

"Seems okay, but you know what it's like."

"Who did this?" she asked Hawksmoor.

The detective shrugged. "No idea so far, Doctor. Till we question the victim."

"Victim?" The strange word made Clare look hard from the policeman to the priest.

"Reverend Watson."

"Where did it happen?"

"In the church lane."

"At this hour?"

"He'd been in there. A parishioner crossing the churchyard saw him doing the cleaning some time earlier, then on the way back, saw him praying." Hawksmoor was apologetic. "That's the last eye-witness evidence we've got so far. He has marks of hobnails on his skin, I believe. Right, Dr. Greig?"

"Dorsum, flanks, chest, shoulders."

"Shouldn't you be trying to find out who the assailants were?"

"Our people are out there now, Doctor. Doing all they possibly can."

"Oh, typical!" She turned back to Andy and the recumbent form of the priest. "Andy, I want him supervised."

"I think we'll have to." Andy pursed his lips. She knew what he meant. He had an innate distrust of ambulances, maintaining that you had to be of virtually Olympic fitness to survive the usual dramatic ambulance rush, memorable as it undoubtedly was for spectators. "I'll go with him. Will you keep an ear out, Clare?" He meant the practises, Fieldham and Beckholt together.

She wavered, passing a hand over her cheek. "Shouldn't I go? Let you get back?"

He looked quizzically at her expression, shook his head. "I've seen him since . . . Comparison between states of consciousness."

He was right. She nodded, feeling helpless, looking down at Shaw. "I'll hold the fort, then." She raised her head. "Andy . . ."

"I'll let you know," he said firmly. "It's better if I go. You think a PA and lateral, if he can stand it?"

"There are so many marks on his chest."

"Exactly what I was thinking."

He nodded. Clare stepped aside for the ambulance men and their stretcher. She heard Andy say deliberately, "Now, chaps. Slowly and safely does it. No drama. A nice quiet country drive to the County Hospital. All right?"

She watched them carry the priest from the room and down to the drive where the ambulance stood, blinking its blue lamp. She stepped past Hawksmoor and Nurse Batsford, and after a moment's pause walked slowly towards the gate. The crowd of spectators shuffled as she approached, it seemed to her almost in anticipation.

"How is he, Doctor?" somebody asked.

"Get out of my way," she said, ice in her voice.

The spectators fell back. In total silence she went to her car and waited stonily until the ambulance emerged and turned with ponderous slowness towards the main Colnebridge road. Andy would be inside, ready to play hell with the driver if he misbehaved. The people watched, talking in undertones.

She wound the car window down. "Have you Beckholt people no homes to go to?" she ripped out.

Then she fired the engine and drove slowly home.

CHAPTER 26

Moments later Shaw Watson recovered consciousness in the ambulance.

"You were knocked about," Andy Greig told him. "Remember?"

"Yes." The priest kept his eyes closed after a moment's dazed stare at the police constable, the doctor and the vehicle's interior.

"You're in an ambulance."

"Hospital?"

"Afraid so," the doctor said, wondering why he should be feeling so apologetic. "Possibly only a day. Depends."

"Who did it?" the constable asked.

"I don't know. I was coming from the church."

"How many, Reverend?"

"I couldn't tell. Three, I think."

The constable wrote laboriously. "Time?"

"It was dark."

Dr. Greig signalled to the constable, who obediently put his pocket book away.

"You rest, Reverend. We'll be having a look at you in Casualty."

Shaw's eyes opened. "Might I ask . . . ?"

"Me? I'm Dr. Greig. Fieldham." A thought occurred. "One thing. Do you remember being found?"

"A dog. Was it Alan's?"

"That's right. He said you spoke, told him not to get Dr. Salford. Remember?"

"Did I?" The priest shifted his position under the blanket, grunting with the pain.

"Why?"

"I can't quite . . . She's too close to it all. The villagers could make a lot of trouble for her . . ."

"I see." Dr. Greig remembered Clare's expression when she'd arrived at the rectory. "Rest," he said. "We're nearly there."

"I'm sorry to be a bother."

"No bother. Rest."

That Thursday's well-baby clinic functioned with the slick accuracy of a Jesuit mass, and in almost total silence.

"She's *terrible*," Jackie hissed furtively at Mrs. Locking after shooing in the merry three-month-old Belmont baby.

The cleaner was up in arms. "You know what she said to me when I come in?"

"Wonder she spoke at all." The receptionist felt she'd borne the brunt and whatever it was it couldn't possibly have been worse than what she herself was having to endure.

Mrs. Locking grumbled on. "I says, Good morning, Doctor! and she gives back, 'Late again, Mrs. Locking?' Me! Never been late in my life!"

"Yes, well," Jackie sniffed, who knew the truth of it. "You can escape, Mrs. Locking, once you've skipped round. I'm in the thick."

"Whatever's up with her?"

"It's Reverend Watson," the receptionist said wisely. "Upset her."

"Here." Mrs. Locking checked that the mothers in the waiting-room were occupied in a muted chatter. "You don't think there's anything—well—*there*, do you?"

"Oh no." Jackie was decided. "Nothing like that. She can't stand him. No time for religion and suchlike. Only last week she was on about it."

"Anyway, I heard she goes about with somebody from Colnebridge."

"Who?"

"Really handsome, so I heard. She's been seen in his car."

"I keep hoping about Dr. Greig," Jackie said. "I think he's lovely."

"Think about him later, Jackie Hughes. You'd better hurry to Doctor." Mrs. Locking had seen the reception signal light go on, and was duly gratified when the receptionist, squeaking in alarm, rushed off with an armful of files. Skip round, indeed.

She wondered if she dared risk a cigarette but decided not with Dr. Salford in such a mood. Smoke lingered so. Last time she'd been caught there'd been real trouble. She went into the waiting-room to see the babies. There'd be time to do the corridor after a bit of a natter, with luck.

Old Stan watched morosely from his chair in the cottage doorway. Hilda Winner had made the killer some sandwiches to take to work again. And the killer had taken them, spoken briefly with the woman and waved at her from the lane.

"Cosy little scene it's becoming," he said aloud.

There was payment there. He was sure of that. Women were no different from men, not deep down. They didn't go to all that trouble for nothing. Baked again yesterday. Not asked her dear old friend Mr. Deller over. Oh dear no. Only the killer. A killer who could repay her kindness with . . . with whatever she found most rewarding. A really satisfying (no other word would do) payment. Women were animals, animals. Look at that harlot Davidson.

Strange how evil attracted women. Moths to a flame, a woman to horror and evil. Some extraordinary thrill that friendship and peace could not provide. But that only showed their own base nature. Base. Like that evil killer's nature.

Last night, after reporting back to his dear and new-found lady-friend next door, the killer had gone to sit in his house. Again his sinister nature showed, sitting in the gathering dusk without bothering to put the lamp on until very late, almost midnight. Hilda Winner had left her porch light on and occasionally moved casually about behind her front room curtains. But they couldn't fool him, not old Stan. Shadows could be very deceptive. They were keeping up the pretence that there was still only the front lane entrance into their respective gardens, but evil was clever, clever. There were ways round *that* little problem.

"Especially if a kind lady wants to see her dear young killer friend urgently," he said aloud to no one. "For very personal reasons."

She was becoming a harlot. That was the truth of it. Not too uncharitable to face up to the truth. The killer was a real one for harlots, wasn't he? First Olive Hanwell, then wheedling a job through that other harlot Joan Davidson down in Saints Brook valley woods so well protected by her tame-kept savage who masqueraded as her foreman—and now getting his feet under Hilda Winner's table by his evil ways.

Of course she'd enticed him by her own disgusting wiles.

Anybody could tell what she was up to, just by looking. Filth, filth.

Clare's clinic ended on time. She called to Jackie as the last patient was leaving. Baby Queen, screaming with laughter, was successfully weighed, palpated, measured, evaluated and returned to its re-educated mother in its carrycot, guilty of being found yet again fit as a flea.

"Mrs. Hughes! Where is Mrs. Locking?"

Jackie was instantly nervous at the tone. "She's doing the corridor, Doctor."

"Tell her I want to see her."

"Yes, Doctor."

Clare waited, drumming her fingers. As the cleaner entered she cut loose. Out in the reception area, an aghast Jackie Hughes heard every word. After hearing one brief exchange, Mrs. Queen scrambled her hilarious infant out of the surgery as fast as she could go.

"Mrs. Locking," Clare began coldly, hardly letting the woman get in the room. "This surgery is a discredit to my profession. Because of your idleness."

"Beg pardon, Doctor?" Mrs. Locking fended, her ingratiating smile stiffening.

"Disgusting. Dirty. Repellent. Filthy. On account of your indolence. You take the money—"

"Dr. Salford! I won't be spoke to like this—!"

"You *will*, you idle old fraud!" Clare's quiet tone sliced through the cleaner's expostulations. "You take your unearned wages every single week, having earned barely one-tenth of what you have been paid. I'm no longer prepared to tolerate your uselessness. Do I make myself clear?"

"But I come here regular as clockwork, never miss a single day—"

"You are a fraud, Mrs. Locking, taking wages for work not done. Of course you turn up each day. And you've never been on time since I came. You are lazy, idle, practically useless."

"Dr. *Salford!*"

"Lazy. And hypocritical. I've been ashamed, on too many occasions to mention, of the dirt you leave around. You won't do it again, Mrs. Locking. Not here."

Mrs. Locking's voice wavered as she frantically decided to bend before the storm. "I do try my best, Doctor."

"You malinger, Mrs. Locking. Just go away. You'll get a week's wages for notice."

The cleaner's voice hardened viciously. "You can't do that! There's the employment law—"

"Sue me," Clare said flatly. "Please leave." She belled the receptionist. Mrs. Locking turned to watch Jackie come, stunned by the speed of her dismissal. "Mrs. Hughes. I've dismissed our so-called cleaner for providing totally unsatisfactory services. Please record it as dismissed for "idleness, unpunctuality and lack of cleaning ability." Tell her to leave this instant."

Jackie drew an aghast breath, but Mrs. Locking was already making a belligerent exit.

"You'll hear more of this!" she snapped.

"Not as much as you will, Mrs. Locking," Clare said calmly.

"And I'll change my doctor!"

"I'll insist on that."

"And see you never get another cleaner from the village!"

"So shall I. Anyway," Clare barbed neatly, feeling pleasure in the retort. "I've never had one yet, have I? *Leave!*"

Departing angrily two minutes later, Mrs. Locking almost bumped into Mrs. Horn on the surgery steps. She clumped past without a word.

The leader of the Guild of Village Wives had chosen her moment well. The period immediately following the well-baby clinic was always fallow, with few interruptions since there was no telling exactly how long a clinic would continue. She had waited on the playing fields, sitting on the long Coronation bench seats and counting the mothers who emerged. Mrs. Queen the last. She exchanged a word with the young mother and admired her uproarious infant then, guessing that Jackie Hughes would not be leaving yet awhile, she marched into the surgery.

The receptionist was apprehensively tidying the records away behind her barriered alcove.

"I want to see Dr. Salford, Jackie."

"You have no appointment, Mrs. Horn." Jackie began a frantic search through the appointments book, fearful of some omission. Mrs. Horn smiled grimly.

"One won't be necessary. She'll see me. It's personal."

Jackie felt exhausted. The day was becoming a bewilderment."

"Just tell her it's about a certain police officer."

"Wait, please."

Clare was finishing tidying her instruments away when the receptionist appeared and announced that Mrs. Horn was waiting.

"It's personal. She said you'd see her."

"Not just now, Jackie. I've something on."

Jackie fidgeted. "Doctor. She said to tell you it's about a police officer."

Clare did not look away from the instrument case. She was careful to carry on going through the top layer, replacing indispensables with concentration. So it had happened at last. She and Ken. They had found out. She had few illusions left now about Beckholt's true nature. They had *found* out, worked hard at it until the invaluable nugget of information was exposed, to be used for their own foul ends and spent to buy service and obedience. Not even Danegeld. It was to be the price of a mercenary ally, and she was to be enlisted as that mercenary.

After an appreciable moment she looked up as if still preoccupied. "Yes?"

"Mrs. Horn." Jackie began to explain again. "She said you'd see her if I said it was about a police officer."

"And what did I reply?"

Clare gazed around to check all was in order and took up her handbag. Jackie swallowed and withdrew to confront Mrs. Horn uncertainly.

"Doctor's too busy to see you just now, Mrs. Horn. If you'd care to—"

"Oh, *is* she?"

"Yes, she is." Clare emerged, turning to shut the consulting-room door.

Mrs. Horn stepped forward angrily. "I have something to tell you, Doctor. In strictest confidence."

Clare passed the keys for Jackie to hang on the board. "I don't wish to share your confidences, Mrs. Horn."

"You will, Doctor. And I suggest you ask Mrs. Hughes to leave before I speak!"

"I won't, Mrs. Horn. And I suggest *you* leave *my* surgery." Clare scribbled in the reception notepad. "I'll be at the County Hospital seeing a patient, Jackie. Male surgical."

"Very well, Doctor," Jackie said weakly in the crossfire.

Mrs. Horn felt the situation slipping out of her grasp, and tried desperately. "About your *friend.*"

Clare found her car keys and told Jackie, "Lock up here, please. I'll leave through the house." She moved past the belligerent visitor, adding, "I'm sure we have no friends in common, Mrs. Horn."

"Your friend the inspector!" Mrs. Horn exclaimed in desperation.

"Jackie," Clare said in a matter-of-fact voice, "get rid of this hysterical woman, would you, please. And return her cards. She's not a patient of mine from today."

"You can't do that!" Mrs. Horn exclaimed furiously. "It's five miles to the next surgery!"

"I assure you I can," Clare asserted. "Patients can choose a doctor—and vice versa."

Mrs. Horn's reserve broke and the hatred spilled out. "You wicked woman!"

"I'll be an hour, Jackie." Clare pushed past.

"Whoring! With a married man! And you a doctor, too!"

Clare spoke with maddening calm to the receptionist. "Call me if this old woman becomes violent, will you? They can bleep me from the County switchboard."

"It's you that lets this murderer stay here!"

Clare swung round, claws out. "Does it not occur to you, Mrs. Horn, that if the law is correct and Taunton *is* innocent, then *you* did it?"

"Did . . . ?"

"Yes. That *you* murdered Olive Hanwell?"

"*Me?* How dare you!"

"You. Or George Falconer. Or Eric Carnforth. Or Jenny Tree. Or Mick Robie, or Hilda Winner, or any of you." She advanced on Mrs. Horn, who took a step away. "But *one* of you, Mrs. Horn. Not an incomer. You Beckholt people." She saw the woman struggle to find an argument and continued remorselessly. "Not one of *us* incomers, Mrs. Horn. *You.* It seems," she concluded, feeling sadder than she could remember, "that Beckholt people murder their own."

She turned away then and slid the intervening door on them both.

"It's Saturday. We get him then."

"Right, Mick. I'll be there. When he comes home from work we'll be at the cottage—"

"We won't." Mick was even more decisive than usual.

"During the night, like?" Joe Robie asked his cousin. They were gathered in a group at one end of the social club. It had not yet filled up for the evening. Apart from a few children sitting with their parents it was safe, with enough noise from the juke-box to drown any conversation.

"No. While the pubs are still open." Mick grinned at their faces.

"Then how are we covered?" Bob Barber asked, worried by Mick's idea. "We can't speak for each other. They won't have that."

"Not they. But there's a fishing competition on the Bures river."

"And we enter?"

"Yes. Night fishing, half-eight start. That gives us time to reach our pegs, set up rods."

"But the other anglers'll see us leave."

"They would, Frank," Mick corrected him, "if we hadn't planned it different. See." He drew them closer with a jerk of his head. "We get two of us on the outside markers. The rest of us are in between, see? Say there's seven of us. Well the outside two stay put, fish like mad. The middle five slip off, like. Nobody knows they're gone, right? Soon as the match gets going. The pegs are set a hell of a way apart."

"It's risky," Frank muttered. "They might check."

"And the pegs are chosen by lot, drawn out of a hat before the competition."

"You're bleedin' thick," Mick Robie told Bob scornfully. "Think I can't fix a little thing like that? You must think I'm a daft bugger."

"I've never been fishin'." Ned smiled uneasily.

"Then you can come wi' me," Mick promised. "In a car we leave by the roadside."

"Why don't we just collar him at work?" Frank suggested.

"Because Bertie'll be sniffin' around the Hall Farm." Mick shrugged. "I'm not scared o' the bugger, but I seed him break Jensen's back in the wrastlin' two fairs agone. I'll not cross Bertie, not for a gold clock."

"Nor me," Joe agreed fervently. "Tell you straight, I'm frit o' the man."

"Then in his cottage?" Frank persisted.

"Not there, either. We done it once. Joe Sheldon's always on the prowl, worse'n a bloody poacher these nights."

"In the pub?"

"You'm thick-headed, Ned. No. We gets him just as he comes i' the village. He always come tippen up the footpath to the bottom of his gantway. It'll be past mucklight by then."

"How'll we know that?"

"I know that," Joe answered. "He'm marsh cuttin' still. Saturday night he'll be finishin' the Saints Brook. Reached the copse, the old ruin by then." His tone became embittered. "He'm a tightly worker."

"And only Sparrow on," Mick checked with his cousin. "For them girt cows."

"Only him." Joe gave a short bark of laughter. "Not me, that's for sure."

"And there's a special on down the Hall Farm. Right, Joe?"

"Mmmm. Mrs. Davidson's throwin' some party. A few folk comin'. Mucklight'll see 'em all swillin' away."

"So." Mick gazed around them. "No better night for a quiet bit o' fishin', lads. And it's weekend. Jannock?"

"It's jannock a'right," Frank said slowly in wonderment.

"It's good," Ned smiled. "It's somethin' for nothin'. No chance o' gettin' caught."

"And *he* gets netted for sartin."

"You'm woundly clever, Mick." Ned's smile grew broader than ever.

CHAPTER 27

For Clare it had seemed a sterile end to the week. She went through the clinics like a zombie, listlessly answering calls, paying scant attention to Jackie's anxious chatter and having to flog herself into showing medical interest.

The visit to check on Shaw Watson had been a waste. The pathetic man had been embarrassed, slightly woozy still but desperate to make ordinary conversation with his visitor. She had found herself behaving coldly clinical in an attempt to cover her embarrassment. The fool of a man had been more concerned to put her at ease than tell her of his own worries. "I'll be fine," he'd said trustingly. "They'll let me out tomorrow or the next day."

"To return to Beckholt?" she had asked distantly. "With all that entails?"

"Where else would I go?"

"Anywhere else. Don't you regard what happened as a threat? A warning? Any reasonable person would."

"It's my home now."

"A dangerous one. For you."

"Two or three tearaways aren't them all."

"Who would give evidence against them?" Clare found her

animosity towards him lessening for the first time. Perhaps it was finding him in a hospital bed, sixth of a line of beds down one sterile side, obedient to the instructions of anyone medical. Perhaps it was the spectacle of his injuries. His scalp lacerations were covered, his hands wrapped with one thumb splinted. Mercifully no other bone was fractured. The temporal swelling had proved a simple haematoma.

He noticed her inspection and misunderstood. He lifted a shoulder to indicate his right ear. "They cleaned it," he explained. "But it seeps, rather, I can't wash it myself yet."

"That's all right." Again that faint embarrassment, as if she'd been caught out at something. "You haven't answered my question. Quite a few villagers must know who attacked you. None's come forward. I asked the police." She avoided saying Ken had told her this.

"Well, even one per cent . . ."

Clare said firmly, "Practically all of them. They're in it. They *know*."

"But they're the parish, my people."

"Is your wonderful religion so poorly organized that it cannot arrange a transfer for you somewhere safer?"

"And leave them to somebody else?" Shaw smiled wearily. "I didn't mean you, Doctor. I meant another priest, brand new and liable to make more mistakes even than me. Which'd be saying something."

"It's because you went to the police," Clare rammed home, feeling the familiar irritation come welling back at the man's stubbornness. "They'll do it again and again, until you'll have to go. You might even be . . ."

"Thanks for your concern, Doctor. But I think of it as a couple of lads having had a few drinks, thinking they'd steal some more of the church silver, panicked and hit out. They're not malicious."

She drew breath. "Your presence is damaging the village. If you left, this Taunton problem would disappear."

"Do you believe that?"

"Yes!" Clare exclaimed. "Yes I do!"

He looked away. "And if I did go, would you agree with that

petition? Help them to bar Taunton completely?"

"That's nothing to do with the point!"

"It has, Clare," he said tiredly. "You'd hold out on your own against them. I'll not leave you to that."

Shocked, she rose from the chair, swiftly gathering her hand-bag and saying, "Martyrdom charges a price." She heard with dismay the slight shake in her voice.

He tried a wry grin. "Nothing as grand as martyrdom for me," he said. "I'd mess it up."

She turned as he started to mouth an apology, for what she did not wait to discover. Let the bloody man do as he pleased, she fumed inwardly, stalking the length of the ward. Somebody should phone the bishop and *make* him leave. I'm a fool to my-self, she thought, slamming angrily into the sister's office. Wor-rying about a religious maniac on one hand and an affluent police officer who had it made on the other.

And I miss out, she thought. Maybe general practice was the wrong job entirely.

She had pondered on her visit during the drive home. Added to it was Nurse Batsford's request the following day for two hours off at the most inconvenient period of the working hours. She said it was an urgent personal matter which couldn't be delayed. Naturally Clare had conceded, only to hear Jackie pass on the message to the nurse that the hire car she'd ordered earlier was on its way from Colnebridge. Clare guessed then it was for Esther to drive to the County Hospital and fetch Shaw Watson. Natural enough, and in any case none of her own business.

And then there'd been three emergency calls during the night, followed by a severe injury to a farm labourer next morn-ing out at Fogg Powell's place near Friday Woods. This inter-rupted the morning surgery and caused such a delay Clare could not finish until well after two that afternoon. What with the calls to make out on the practise and the antenatal clinic from six till seven, and evening surgery to follow at half past, she was exhausted as well as unaccountably depressed. There was a brooding unease in the village. Perhaps that was producing her

autumnal mood of foreboding. She went to bed that night too
tired to sleep.

It was only to be expected that she was called out again, this
time at three o'clock, to resuscitate a sinful old devil of an oc-
togenarian ex-soldier with chronic bronchitis who had gleefully
used the night hours to escape his family and smoke a forbidden
pipe of plug tobacco. Clare hauled him, sullenly unrepentant,
back from his eternal reward by half five and drove home.
Morning surgery was due to start at eight-fifteen.

On her round Clare decided to make her long overdue visit to
Mrs. Seddon. This elderly teacher occasionally did competition
embroidery work. As the subject was one of Clare's interests,
she had a ready excuse.

She found the grey-haired lady setting up her frame for a new
freehand design incorporating countryside symbols. Clare duly
admired the design, commenting on the risky choice of colours,
and entered into a brisk exchange on the texture needed in the
final embroidery.

With difficulty she managed to refuse Mrs. Seddon's insistence on providing tea but exchanged a little innocent gossip.
She told Mrs. Seddon how much she had taken to Monica
James, how pretty she thought she was. Such a pleasantry did
no harm, especially when it reached to the subject herself—as
Clare was sure it would. That safely brought up Les Taunton
and Clare began to delve with all the interrogative skill at her
command.

Eventually she left knowing nothing more than Monica
James had told her. The little lad Badger was normally only of
average disobedience, but had turned sullen in music classes,
causing total disruption by episodic bouts of utter silence,
sulkiness and refusing even to sing with all the class when he
was known to have quite a pleasant alto voice. "Even possibly
absolute pitch," Mrs. Seddon had sighed. "A rarity. But some
children are like that . . ." Worse, she'd been sure that deep
down the boy actually loved music. But there was no account-
ing for children . . .

Nothing new, Clare thought, driving to check on old Elsie Wilson's oedematous legs. Nothing new.

Joe Sheldon took the *County Banner* on Fridays for the local news. He tried to read it in three doses: breakfast, lunch and at tea. Eileen tried to make tea a regular event for the whole family, an increasing difficulty with the children's friends coming round all hours wanting them to play out.

That Friday was particularly hard work. She had to drag every word out of Joe. Usually you could hardly get a word in edgeways.

"You're reading that like for an exam," she jibed.

"Mmmm?"

"Hardly spoken a syllable, love." She indicated the *Banner*. "What are you looking for?"

"Wish I knew," he said, and returned to his search.

She noted uneasily that it *was* a search. He wasn't just reading. It was an intent methodical inspection, inch by inch and every single line.

She started a false, brittle chatter with the children about bicycles while her husband searched remorselessly on.

CHAPTER 28

Clare was surprised at seeing Shaw Watson, having assumed the famous supper parties at Hall Farm were always made up from Colnebridge. The presence of the priest displeased her and his marks of injury proved ever more irritating.

The idea was to have drinks on the long patio before supper.

"You two have met, of course," Mrs. Davidson welcomed her. "This is Bertie. I positively refuse to do that absurd double introduction. We're not in the Regency any more."

Her hostess was not overdressed, Clare saw with relief. And the scandalous Bertie turned out to be a grave, rather taciturn, thickset man obviously accustomed to making decisions. His manner contrasted strongly with that of the priest, who characteristically did not know whether to come forward or wait by his verandah chair as Clare entered. As she accepted a sweet sherry she realized that Shaw and Bertie seemed quite at ease with each other.

"I don't think you've been here before, Clare, have you?" Mrs. Davidson asked, guiding Clare to a scrollwork chair. "Our aim is to get plastered fairly quickly before it's time to eat. That will be quite soon, actually, because I get caterers from town—saves countless friendships. My own cookery is abysmal."

Another guest was announced and Sandra brought Monica James in. The teacher was cool and stylish in a clever green dress of Thai silk with a lovely gold necklet that emphasized her light colouring. The priest was glad to see her, coming forward spontaneously and only faltering at the last moment by not reaching out to take her hand with confidence. Not dithering that time, Clare observed.

"Stop that!" Mrs. Davidson ordered cheerfully. "I'll have no titles or surnames this evening. Christian name for Shaw, and first names for the rest of us pagans. Okay everyone?"

"How sensible. I'll start," Monica James said. "Hello, Shaw, Joan, Clare, Bertie."

"You'll notice there's a plan," their hostess confessed. "I'd better own up before you get the vibes and wonder what I'm about. I'm always truthful when I'll get found out anyway."

"Good gracious!" Clare exclaimed with a smile. "Not those games?"

"Nearly, but not quite, dear." Joan Davidson brought Monica a sherry. "I was so petrified at having people from Beckholt to supper that I waited for an excuse."

"But we're not Beckholtians," Monica countered.

"That's the point!" her hostess shrieked. "Who else would dare brave this scandalous place? Who else is sufficiently tolerant?"

Surprisingly it was Shaw Watson who first laughed aloud. "So you're starting on us. Is that it?"

"Exactly! And I thought we could see who got to learn most gossip about each other—you about my scandalous relationship with Bertie there, or me about you."

"And the excuse?" Clare asked, deciding she liked the scandalous Joan Davidson of Hall Farm.

"Why, this labourer of mine who's turned us topsy-turvy!"

"Of yours?" Monica interposed. "I hadn't heard he worked for you."

"I was positively *preyed* upon by a malicious priest until I repented and saw the light," Joan answered, adding with pretended confidentiality, "I shan't disclose who it was, my dear, but I shall demand an enormous refund in the form of indulgences, or whatever they're called."

Ken arrived into the midst of amused repartee between Shaw Watson and his hostess.

"I'm not irreverent, Shaw," she was asserting when Ken came in. "I just want payment for services rendered."

She maintained a charming patter as the last arrival mixed in. During the introductions Clare detected a growing awareness as Monica's antennae responded to her relationship with the tall man but she was satisfied she was concealing her own interest well. Ken had contacted her as soon as he received the invitation and she was determined to play at being a former casual acquaintance.

"Ken's been here before," Joan announced. "Being from Colnebridge and of its establishment, he's not tarred with the same brush as the rest of you."

"Therefore I'm acceptable by definition." Ken entered into the spirit of things, silently toasting his hostess. "I'm just surprised some of these Beckholt people have actually made it."

"We were inveigled," Monica retorted with spirit.

"Monica's right," Clare agreed. "Each of us was led to believe that only Colnebridge guests were invited."

"Drink up and stop this civil war, all of you!" Joan rushed about dispensing more refreshment. "We must be at least a little wobbly before we dine. These visiting caterers mean you have to eat at a frightful gallop!"

Clare chatted with Monica and Joan about village affairs while the three men talked about farming. She found Joan Davidson's prattle entertaining and Monica was a pleasant companion, but she developed a persistent uncomfortable feeling as the evening got under way. It was that same unease which had been accumulating all week. And despite the friendly babble others seemed to sense it too. Twice, when she had glanced across at the men, where Shaw was smilingly interrogating Bertie about the district's old-fashioned farming methods, she caught Monica looking away from her just in time. And Joan prattled on and on. Despite her apprehension, Clare was soon able to relax and make a good attempt at unconcern. Why not simply enjoy the evening, she lectured herself, and soon actually began to respond.

Joe Sheldon stepped out into the road, waving the two cars down.

"Friggin' 'ell!" Ned's smile hardened at the sight of the helmet. He screeched to a panicky stop, almost causing Frank's car to run into him.

"Take it easy!" Mick Robie snapped. "We're going fishing, remember."

"Off on the razzle, lads?" The police sergeant was quite affable, leaning in on the driver's side.

"Fishin', Joe."

"Where would that be, then? Didn't know you were anglers."

"Up Bures way. Comin'?"

Sheldon grinned and wagged a finger. "I know you lads. You're a boozy lot. You'll put your rods up and slip off somewhere. Like the Crown," he added innocently.

"Not us, Joe." Mick gazed back with just as much innocence. "We're serious anglers. Competition, you see. We'm goin' to win us a few pints tonight."

Ned put in unnecessarily, "They check us every hour, Joe."

"That so?"

"Don't keep us," Mick Robie said. "We've a journey."

"Only seven or eight miles, Mick. It's not far."

"See you, Joe." Ned's smile recovered its cheeriness. "We'll let you know how we get on."

"Good luck. Don't do anything I wouldn't do."

"Cheers, Joe."

Ned let the clutch in. Mick puffed out his cheeks with relief.

"See?" Ned said. "I told you. He's a real glass-arse these days, that Sheldon. He's everywhere."

The policeman watched the cars on to the main road and saw them dwindle northwards. He scanned the clouds, the remaining daylight. They were in good time for the match. It was due to start at eight-thirty. There was a roll-call, usually a registration business followed by a supervised drawing of lots for "pegs," places where an angler was to fish. The distances between pegs varied, sometimes extending to several hundred yards but often less than this. The *Banner* had announced a peg interval of a hundred feet.

He examined the sky again. No wind to speak of and all the swallows leaving or gone. On impulse he got into his panda and drove towards Taunton's cottage, acknowledging the odd wave from villagers out in their gardens enjoying the last of the day. He switched the radio over to the BBC weather forecast. Mist on low ground, fog in coastal areas, cooler temperatures, rain again before dawn. That meant a low night mist crawling up the Bures river to the hamlet before midnight and staying till ten o'clock tomorrow.

Mrs. Winner was sweeping her path when he stepped out and asked after Les Taunton.

"He'll not be back before dusk," she told him confidently. "He's got a long job on. Marshing Saints Brook."

"About what time, Hilda?"

"Oh, later than usual, I suppose. Trying to finish it, he told me. Wanting to prove good this first week, I suppose, though he's always been a late bird."

"Thanks, Hilda." He slid into his panda car, not seeing her concern.

"Is anything wrong, Joe? He's all right, isn't he?"

"No—all fine."

Then he was back on the road and driving home but still worried. The made-up road ran the long way round. A more direct route to Mrs. Davidson's Hall Farm was the footpath from the end of Taunton's lane down to Saints Brook and downstream about a mile. But however you looked, it was a long way from a fishing match near Bures.

CHAPTER 29

Supper was going splendidly. Clare had the tendency of all who live alone to skimp meals, settling for snacks to save time and labour, so she especially enjoyed the stuffed veal. Joan had decided on courgettes aux fines herbes and risked château potatoes with the dish.

The dessert was some concoction she had never tasted before, a pavlova courageously decorated with sliced green kiwi fruit. Monica did battle, explaining that Joan's account of its composition was entirely wrong. Joan airily dismissed the teacher's account— "So much of what I learned at school has proved entirely fallacious, my dear Monica, that I can't possibly let you get away with that absurd description."

She pretended to sulk when the caterer was summoned and his unshakeable summary of the recipe was identical to Monica's. "Yes, Madam, fresh lightly whipped double cream . . ." She threatened the teacher with no liqueurs afterwards as punishment, ending graciously, "Never mind. We've all learned something, haven't we? A teacher can be factually correct . . ." which gave Monica a laugh. Shaw was more relaxed than Clare had seen him, though Ken, who had talked mostly to Monica from his position at the table, was a little mechanical and unlike his true self. Perhaps, Clare wondered, the unease had left herself and flitted into him. But certainly Joan was showing nothing but delight in her guests and Bertie was humourously regaling them with an account of his experiences in the Forces which left the women helpless with laughter. He had found most fascination and humour in the different types one met, he was explaining. Joan said there was no such thing as a standard type of person.

"Differences are my interest," she said, serving the dessert and getting into slight difficulties with the cream. "I'm not quite sober, Shaw," she murmured to him as she served, "but trust me. There actually *is* fruit somewhere under that mound of Bertie's special pasteurized double cream, and all of it will be perfectly fresh—should you actually identify any of it!"

"She likes extremes," Bertie observed, seeing they all had more Krötenbrunnen.

"Who doesn't, darling?" Joan demanded, serving busily. "They're what fascinate all of us, be they in literature, the arts, speech, history. The rest of us are so mundane."

Bertie opened a fresh bottle. "Rubbish. We're all made up of extremes."

"Not in Beckholt," Joan contended. "Same in everything. Our villagers are the absolute in mundanity. We even speak the same—same but different."

"That's true, Bertie." Ken entered the lists. "These locals even have their own dialect, or variation of it."

"All right," Bertie was quite confident he would win this one. "So we call a marsh light a peg o' lantern instead of jack o' lantern. But so does all East Anglia."

"And brock." Clare spoke without thought.

"That's a badger," Bertie explained for Ken's benefit.

"A nickname," Clare added, continuing, conscious of the small silence. "Well, isn't it sometimes a nickname? I heard so."

Monica was looking at her, having passed on this information to her in the first place. Bertie nodded.

"It was Les Taunton's nickname," Joan said without smiling, but keeping her tone light. "I'll have more of that, Bertie. The hostess must drink the dregs herself, especially when there's so much of it. Another bottle, please. I'm sure we can force it down." She smiled sweetly round the table. "You'll have to try to finish off the whole crate, or we'll be having Krötenbrunnen for breakfast for days and *days*."

"Why did they call him that?" Monica asked Joan the question for Clare.

Sandra crept in to call Bertie to the phone. Joan, the only one with true local knowledge, shrugged.

"All I know is a badger eats worms at night."

"And isn't Taunton rather a night bird?" Clare said.

"He was often kept in," Monica said. "But so are many children."

"Not quite as much as Taunton," Ken put in. "It seems to have been a regular thing."

"Well, a child in those days was often kept back to finish what he'd avoided doing during the day." Monica tried not to sound too much like a teacher confronting a dissatisfied parent. "Maybe that's where his name comes from?"

"A late worker," Clare mused. "Forcibly made to *be* a late worker because he couldn't complete his work?"

"Not *couldn't*," Monica said, getting a nod of agreement from Ken. "Wouldn't."

"Regularly?" Shaw asked Monica, and when Monica negated this turned to ask Ken. "You said regular."

"Often," Ken said. "Totalling up to one of the worst in the class for detention."

"Often," Clare said, as if in a dream. "But if you checked the record in detail, Ken, rather than merely add them up for comparison of totals, you'd find the periods of detention are very irregular."

Her mind was screaming, *It adds up! It all adds up!*

"Would I?" Ken said, curious.

"Yes."

There was a pause. They were all looking at Clare in silence. The blood had drained from her face.

And she realized she knew who had killed Olive Hanwell, that Taunton was completely innocent.

She said, "Completely irregular. Some weeks he'd be fine, others in terrible trouble."

"How do you know?"

"Because Taunton's innocent. He always was innocent. Even of those detentions he incurred as a child at school. And innocent of the murder of Olive Hanwell."

Bertie returned into the silence and halted.

"Where's Taunton, Bertie?" Ken demanded.

"Not at home. That was Sergeant Sheldon asking me to look about on the farm for him. He's not at his cottage."

"Where was he last?"

"Cutting on the Saints Brook, towards the ruins. He was to clear it this week."

"Did he get anywhere near finishing?" Clare had risen.

"Yes. He should have done by dusk."

"But if he was delayed," Clare worked out swiftly, "he'd stay to finish, even in dusk?"

Bertie nodded. "He's a trier. Erratic worker, but willing."

"Bertie, remember if you can," Clare instructed. "Has he seemed dreamy, maybe a bit dozy?"

"Why, yes. The first morning. A whole bloody hour, standing staring at the copse where the old ruins stand."

"Ken." Clare rushed to him and urged him to the door. "Call your people. He'll have tried to finish his cutting work in the dusk. Something, some memory of being down there in his youth, will be holding him there. *On his own.*"

"How—?"

"Because he's an epileptic."

"But that was never alleged—"

"Not the grotesque classic kind! Petit mal. And probably generated by music. Usually goes undiagnosed." She was frantic, shouting almost and trying to drive Ken to act.

Bertie ran, dragging open the french windows and bawling out into the darkness for Sparrow to saddle Shakespeare. Shaw ran with him but had the sense to stop and tell Joan to have every light switched on in the house and draw back the curtains. A marker would be needed in the dark.

Les Taunton was running, blundering through the darkness. Instinctive to run downhill, faster that way from the voices of the men chasing. They called occasionally, telling each other where their quarry could be heard threshing through the tangled undergrowth in the valley bottom.

He knew who they were. The same who'd set on his cottage and hit the priest and tried to burn his thatch and killed Hawkeyes. He retched from fear, but kept going. His tiredness had left him the instant they swarmed out: *Get 'im, lads!* The terror was fearsome, frightening. A chase was worse than any capture, the knowledge that you were one and the pack was everyone else and after you. One. The hunted was never plural, always one. The hunters were everyone, everyone in the whole world.

He screamed with pain as a bramble tore his eye. For a second he staggered to a halt, pressing the heel of his palm against his injured eye, then remembered he had to keep going and ran blindly on. They were closer, scrambling down the field and through the hedge after him. He ran with his eye screwed tight in agony, down across the field, afraid his sobbing breath would be audible. The little river was a hundred yards off. Instinctively again he found himself turning right, the way he knew best. That was where he'd hidden so often in games as a child. *But so had they.*

From their shouts they were spreading over the field to prevent his doubling back in the darkness. Packs always did that. He'd been part of a pack once, a beagling pack with dogs chasing small desperate hares across open land. There were thickets, down and to the right. He missed his footing as he blundered on, slipped and splashed into the water.

"Over here, lads!" Mick's great voice. "I heard 'im!"

"Down the water!"

The fugitive scrambled back up the bank, found the high grass. A hundred or so yards further on and his way would be clear. He could cut across the river there, making any noise he cared to, then a straight stretch up the opposite slope of the valley and out over the last dairy fields to Hall Farm's perimeter and safety, blissful safety, for there ran the main road to link a couple of miles off with the London highway. Always full of traffic, night and day, and traffic police in the lay-bys . . .

A yell came from behind him. And two answered, on the fields the other side of the river. On the other, the uphill slope. *In front?* He stopped, gasping, trying to listen.

"Go royt, bu-oys!"

"A'right, Mick!"

They'd gone round that way too. Sent two or even more to wait in case he'd cut and run. He'd twisted in their grip like an eel and escaped, but only into a trap. No lamps, of course. Countrymen needed no lamps to suss their path for them, especially chasing a frightened quarry across countryside they knew so well. And the hunted creature always made every mistake from terror, knowing his fate. He ran on, head down in agony from his torn eye, but wearily and with a growing sense of doom, towards the only place he could cross the river now. The old plank ford. The shouts from behind and across the river grew nearer. It was useless. Why not stop, try to swim in the shallows? Or try hiding under the bank? But a man, in a narrowed river barely entitled to the name, was as good as caught. His breath was going, his side stitching badly and his throat raw.

He could see the car headlights from the main London road as he shambled forward. Those people in the cars didn't know the lads were in full cry after him, that soon he would be kicked to a gruesome death in a field to be found by some sheepdog in the early mists.

The mists. He'd seen them begin to form in the chilling night air as he had stacked the last of the reeds down by the thickets where the old church ruins stood. He'd started on the opposite bank only a few days ago when Bertie gave him the job. He ducked low, almost afraid to hope, and laboriously ran across the field tangential to the river's curve. He slowed, nearing the tangled growth of the copse and fearing another injury. He needed silence now, though, more than sight—at least until dawn. Instinctively, he went to earth.

He bent lower and moved into the undergrowth, pulling the briars and sloe thorns off his jacket rather than noisily ripping himself free of their hold, and forced himself deeper into the copse. Sometimes a pace carried him only a few inches, but every inch was time gained to dawn. He heard something shuffle nearby, down and to his left, and paused breathlessly guessing it to be a badger on its night perambulation.

The old ruined church up ahead was practically in the thicket's centre. They couldn't come at him from every direction and could move no faster than he through the dense undergrowth. He tried to stop breathing so harshly. That Ned, if he was with them, was a real poacher wise in the lore of night work, and his friend Bob was almost as good. A small animal crashed away, startled.

The shouts were still coming from the direction of the river. He proceeded more steadily, deeper and deeper into the thicket. The night animals had fled at the approach of a different animal, he thought in bitter despair. Maybe the thickets could hide him from his own kind. Silently he wormed nearer to the old church ruins.

Sparrow saddled Shakespeare at speed. The horse, with the obstinacy of its kind, blew out its barrel until Sparrow kneed it to force the girths down tightly. He was cursing and telling the beast off as he trotted it into the stableyard. Bertie practically ran on to the saddle. He carried a handlamp, its krypton bulb emitting a concentrated beam several hundred feet.

"I'm coming!" Shaw ran up.

"Grab hold, Shaw." Bertie indicated his stirrup and Shaw hung on, and urged the big hunter to a rapid trot.

Clare urgently called to Sparrow, but the little Fieldham man was hurrying through the shippons in obedience to Bertie's shouted instructions to rouse the two gamekeepers at the old railway end of Saints Brook and send them along the other bank.

She saw Ken's car swing out and raced through the diningroom to the front drive. Monica was already entering Ken's passenger side. Clare flung herself into the rear seat, angry at having gone the wrong way.

"Any more coming, Clare?"

"No."

Ken swung out on to the Colnebridge road. "Sheldon's going down the lane to the Brook. Bertie'll be all right following the near bank. I'll take the far bank. Either of you know if a car can reach the Saints Brook from the Fieldham road?"

"I should think so," Monica said. "The field has an even slope. We take the children rambles."

"Bertie said Taunton stood almost an hour near the ruins," Clare said. "Something there. He might run that way if he's being chased."

"Who killed her, Clare?"

"I'll guess Mr. Deller. Taunton arranged to meet Olive, maybe down at his cottage. She sees no light burning, and it's so dark. She does the most natural thing in those circumstances, crosses over to the neighbour."

"But why Deller, and not Hilda?" Ken asked.

"Maybe the old man could seem more sympathetic. Maybe Olive thought Hilda Winner would disapprove."

"Why did Taunton sit so long in the dark, though, all those hours?"

"Petit mal's commonest precipitant is music," Clare explained. "I should have thought of it the minute you mentioned his dismissal from music classes. They go into a brown study, sometimes for long periods. Naturally fond of music, the poor man probably switches on the radio when getting home and is triggered into a petit mal when certain music is broadcast. He'd hear nothing, see nothing. Just *be* there."

"Can it be tested?"

"Yes, Ken. Find out what broadcasts were on, the evening Olive was killed. He can be triggered by it."

"We *did* check the broadcasts. Detective-Sergeant Hawksmoor gave evidence. Taunton could remember hearing none of the broadcasts named."

"Of course he couldn't." Clare looked at the night flying past the car windows. "He was mentally a million miles away. The music is the stimulus."

"An instant daydream?" Monica asked.

"But one out of control, that comes unbidden and completely takes over."

"All this might be a false alarm," Monica said reassuringly.

"But possibly not," Ken said, tight-lipped.

"If it is," Monica said lightly, "we can go back and finish that wine."

She wasn't smiling, and nobody answered.

The ruins were more overgrown than Les remembered. Brambles and weeds everywhere, a few sloes and some hawthorn. He crouched beside a pile of stones. It was where the altar would have been if the ancient church still remained.

He remembered that it was near here where Olive and he had made love, to his utter wonder and amazement. She had turned the radio on and they listened and loved. A pretty girl, Olive. But then all women were pretty, attractive. Lovely. Like Hilda Winner who was so kind and like Dr. Salford who was so ratty and like Nurse Batsford who only had eyes for the Reverend. Mostly pretty and friendly, though unpredictable . . .

His breathing was easing. He remembered Olive's jokes and the great good humour she brought to their love-making. Maybe that was all love-making was, good humour between a man and a woman . . . But no. It was violence, sheer violence. In the orgasm there was not a single second left for friendship or compassion. It was sheer violence, savagery fetched home between two linked creatures in their coupling. It was savage, hard.

Violence. Maybe it was a little death. Certainly it was for the man afterwards, though the woman talked and dreamed at ease and replete. The man took a small death. He was alone and expended. Then, in that sad moment of despair, a loving woman could make him hers for life by letting herself show a little compassion and feeling. You could throw away all the fondness that existed before. Crouching still, he began to remember the music from Olive's radio that day they had loved . . .

"Thanks for waiting, Badger," a voice breathed in his ear, and hands took hold of him. "Now's your own finish, the way you did for Olive."

Shaw ran blindly, the few glimpses of blacks and dark greys blurred from his running. He learned as the stitch grew in his left side to favour it and ease the pain by casting his weight on the stirrup-leather to which he clung. At first he was afraid the added weight would impede the great hunter in some way but it moved its massive bulk oblivious of the priest struggling and rasping alongside. After that his second wind came and they covered the ground at speed, the hunter trotting easily and Shaw running with long assisted strides. He had once been a moderate cross-country runner and desperately used all the tricks he knew for saving wind.

"We're close!" Bertie snapped. Shaw heard a shout in the darker void below. Bertie reined in and stood high listening. "There. The ruins!"

He rode on at a gallop, the sudden acceleration almost dragging Shaw off his feet. For a few paces Shaw held on, then was cast off by the breathtaking force of the hunter's powered spurt. He caught his balance and ran on after the mounted man. Bertie had switched the lamp on now. The sudden light showed the thickets round the ruins and the hunter moving across the field away from the river and upwards at a dead run. Bertie was shouting and waving signals with the beam.

Shaw cut across the field, wheezing badly now and feeling his stitch, as Bertie reined in on the edge of the thicket, then rode uphill further to gain ground. Shaw was puzzled but obediently slogged after him until the reason for the horseman's change of direction became obvious. From the higher ground the interior of the copse could be seen. Bertie reined in and shone the hand-lamp downhill to pick out the ruins.

"You've got Taunton!" Shaw heard Bertie yell. "Let him go. I know who you are!"

"Go home to your woman, Bertie!"

"I'll break you, Mick Robie! And that cousin o' yourn!" Bertie yelled back.

"Leave us alone! We'm doin' right!"

"The police are here, on the other side o' the river!"

"So what? No witnesses to what we done."

"We know you!"

"So?" There was a silence. They were probably deciding what their line would be.

"Shall I try to go in?" Shaw asked breathlessly, plodding up. "You keep them talking and I'll—"

"Don't," Bertie ordered tersely. "They'd hear you a mile away. Soon as you step into that lot they'll know straight away and kill him and be off."

"We'll say we found him dead!" Mick's voice bawled.

A car's headlights came erratically closer, approaching down the opposite side of the valley across the hayfield. Its horns sounded three long blasts. Shaw thought, that's Ken.

"Them's the police, lads!" Bertie yelled. "I'll break your backs, and they'll clink the lot o' you."

Jeers erupted from the ruins below. "He'll get it first, and you'll not see us do it!"

Bertie signalled with the lamp. The car drew closer and stopped at the far bank of the river. A figure ran across the headlights towards the plank bridging and towards the thicket. Bertie yelled the situation.

"You in there!" Ken's voice shouted. "I'm Inspector Young. Have you got the man Taunton?"

"Get stuffed."

"He didn't kill Olive Hanwell. We have proof."

"Balls. We know he did. You'll tell us anything."

"Mick!" Shaw found himself shouting. "Mick Robie!"

"We'm got no names in here!" came back, amid laughter.

"This is Reverend Watson, from the church."

"Come for your collection?" Roars accompanied the sally.

"That's consecrated ground you're on. All of it. It's still a church."

"It doesn't look like one from here!"

No laughter now, Shaw told himself.

"It's still a church," he shouted back. "Consecrated ground. That's why it's a thicket still. Nobody can farm it, use it. Not forever."

There was silence. Bertie shone the lamp steadily, standing in the stirrups for greater height. Shaw glimpsed the pallor of a face.

He shouted, "You can't do anything to Taunton in there. It's . . . it's sanctuary."

"We did *you* over—"

The jeer was cut off suddenly as if the shouter had been forcibly gagged.

"That wasn't murder!" Shaw bawled down into the thicket. Breath was a problem.

Ken started to shout again but Bertie waved the hand beam at the distant figure to silence him. Two more cars started downhill from the main road skirting the far side of the valley.

"Is he all right, Mick Robie?" Shaw shouted.

The beam wavered as Shakespeare shifted his weight. Bertie clucked in irritation and found the reins again.

"We done nothin' to 'im, Reverend. He's here."

"Then come on out. Leave him there unharmed."

There was a long pause, some faint noises from the undergrowth. A police constable panted up to stand by the big hunter. Several torches were illuminating the thicket now and more police cars blinking blue rotating lamps were congregating on the hillside.

"All right. We're coming. We done nothin' to 'im." A pause. "All right?"

"All right," Shaw yelled. Suddenly dizzy, he walked away and stood uncertainly to one side feeling slightly sick. He heard the movements from below.

"They're there," the constable exclaimed. The police ringing the thickets closed in on the emerging figures, who stood blinking in the strong lights.

CHAPTER 30

By two in the morning the depositions had been taken and statements signed. And Joan Davidson had seen them all off with thanks.

"Please note that I can't quite promise to arrange such excitement on *every* occasion," she told them, still dazzling.

Out among their respective cars Monica said to Clare in an undertone, "I wonder how coincidental it really was?" She was only half joking, which made Clare, too, wonder.

Shaw had walked from the rectory to Hall Farm so there was some bargaining as to who would give him a lift home. Joan reappeared to organize them, "Clearly, Monica must be saddled with the clergy. Clare on the other hand will be responsible for bringing him tomorrow for tea—"

"Er, Joan," Shaw said apologetically. "I'm, er, busy. Sunday, you see. The service."

"Oh. Still goes on, does it? With that repellent cheap altar wine?" She tutted to Bertie in exasperation. "Why *doesn't* the man serve a light Madeira and double his congregation? Better be Monday, both of you. Four o'clock."

Bertie stood by the gate to give them a wave. Ken looked at Clare and they got into their cars.

Monica reminded Shaw about his seat-belt before flashing her beam to signal good night and driving off. "Tired, Shaw?"

"A little?"

"I'm exhausted." She was watching him too casually. "How strange, to see our hypothesis upset."

He strove to pay attention. "What hypothesis?"

"That we live in a modern world. All the forces of law, Ken and his cops, plus medical science, plus Bertie's physical threat,

couldn't rescue that poor man. But you got him out unscathed."

"They just listened to reason."

Monica laughed and took a hand off the wheel long enough
to lay it gently on his arm. "So your activity is modern too. Of
course. Forgive me, Shaw."

"Well, isn't it?" he demanded, coming out of his torpor.

"You know, I really believe you may be right!"

Ken thought he could legitimately park in the surgery drive for
an hour in view of the night's activities. Clare didn't bother to
put her car away and corrected him as he made to get out.

"Don't come in, Ken. Please."

He looked up from his driving seat. "All right, Clare. But is it
still okay? Us?"

"I suppose so."

He tried for briskness. "You did a good job, diagnosing Les
Taunton out of the stigma of being a murderer. And old
Deller's in the clink."

"He'll get off."

"Will he? He's admitted your story's correct."

"But he never sticks to his diet, mistimes his insulin. He's up
and down like a yoyo. Counsel can claim he was disorientated
on account of a hypoglycaemic state. Low blood sugar makes
you do odd things."

"Like some of these epilepsies?"

"Different pathology. Different mechanism."

"Makes me wonder if we're not just all biochemistry or
pathologies," Ken said. "No abnormal biochemistry means no
crime. But then maybe there'd be no love as well." He'd intended it as a flippant crack but he sensed her immediate with-
drawal. He had said the wrong thing.

She said, "Don't you start, Ken. Look, I'll phone you tomorrow."

"When?"

She shrugged. "When I've time."

Indoors, she buzzed the exchange and switched the phone
through. In the bath minutes later she thought over Ken's

remark. Taunton's rescue was a technological failure, and a success for that ditherer round the corner. The ditherer who had been determined to stay in the village so she would not be the only one left to defend Taunton. How utterly pathetic—a triumph for mumbo-jumbo over law, medicine, the whole of society. A fluke. It must be a fluke. And him so *weak*, so pathetically uncertain of every bloody thing on earth. It all went to show how backward an entire village could be even in this modern age. The stupid weak man.

"Rectory, safe and sound."

"You're very kind." He groaned at the ache as he swung from his seat.

Monica tutted. "No wonder. You must have run like the wind."

"The horse did it all." He shut the door, leant down. "I've enjoyed this evening. Really."

"And it's all come right?" She was smiling mischievously. "Not likely, Shaw. The village will take ages to get over this. Look. I've two tickets for a choral concert next week. Would you like to come?"

"Er, well, thank you. That'd be . . . but would Mr. James . . . erm . . . ?"

She decided for him. "It's all perfectly proper. I'll call round and say which evening."

"Well, thanks, erm, Monica. I look forward—"

"Good night, Shaw." She rubbed his hand with her finger. He withdrew quickly and raised an awkward hand.

"Good night."

She left him then, thinking how uninviting that massive lonely rectory looked. She must find out the date of that choral concert, and somehow get two tickets as soon as possible . . .

Clare went to bed and lay awake for a moment. She now knew what she would do. She'd stay here in this complicated tangle of a village. Maybe she'd double up the practise as Andy Greig wanted, get it better organized. And keep on seeing Ken? Possibly, though there was this awful sensation of things having

changed irrevocably as a result of the night's frantic disorders.
And maybe because of that stupid, weak man. She sighed wearily and began to slip into sleep. On Monday she'd have to endure his company at tea, and probably give him a lift to Hall
Farm and back. Joan Davidson had seen to that.

It was beginning to look as if she was going to have the
wretched priest for life . . .

GRAHAM GAUNT is the pseudonym of a British doctor who lives in East Anglia. *The Incomer* is his first novel for the Crime Club.